FATHOMLESS

JACKSON
PEARCE

LITTLE, BROWN AND COMPANY
New York   Boston

Little, Brown and Company

Hachette Book Group
237 Park Avenue, New York, NY 10017
Visit our website at www.lb-teens.com

Little, Brown and Company is a division of Hachette Book Group, Inc.
The Little, Brown name and logo are trademarks of Hachette Book Group, Inc.

The publisher is not responsible for websites (or their content) that are not owned by the publisher.

First Edition: September 2012

Library of Congress Cataloging-in-Publication Data

Pearce, Jackson.
    Fathomless / by Jackson Pearce.—1st ed.
        p. cm.
    Summary: Celia, who shares mental powers with her triplet sisters, finds competition for a handsome boy with Lo, a sea monster who must persuade a mortal to love her and steal his soul to earn back her humanity.
    ISBN 978-0-316-20778-2 (hc) / ISBN 978-0-316-23244-9 (International)
    [1. Supernatural—Fiction.   2. Sea monsters—Fiction.   3. Sisters—Fiction.
4. Triplets—Fiction.   5. Ocean—Fiction.]   I. Title.
    PZ7.P31482Fat 2012
    [Fic]—dc23

                                                                                2012008425

10 9 8 7 6 5 4 3 2 1

RRD-C

Printed in the United States of America

To my maternal grandparents,
for taking me to tame beaches,
and my paternal grandparents,
for taking me to wild ones

PROLOGUE

There are lights at the surface.

Lights so unlike the sun, that can't reach down into the depths of the ocean. Lights we can see only when we look outside the water. She turned the thought over and over in her mind, imagining the lights as best she could until she had to ask her sisters for help again.

"What about the carnival? Are the lights *on* the rides? What are the rides?" she asked one of the oldest, who just turned away—that sister rarely spoke anymore. Lo sighed, turning back to one of the younger ones, whose first trip to the surface was more recent. "Tell me, Ry?"

"Lights. Lights everywhere, I think on the rides. I don't know what the rides are called anymore," Ry said, sounding irritated at the notion of lights. "And noise. Really, Lo, it's nothing to be excited about. It's not the way you remember it."

That was what they kept telling her—it wouldn't be the way she remembered it. Because the last time she saw the human world, she was human.

She walked on land and sat in the sun and sometimes went so far inland, she couldn't even see the ocean. These were things she barely remembered, things that felt like dreams and grew fainter and fainter each day she spent underwater with her new sisters.

The girls here weren't her real sisters, but sometimes she convinced herself they were. When they streaked through the water, laughing, minds linked by some sort of electric current that skipped through the ocean, when they'd been under so long that they forgot a human world existed...then they were her real sisters, her real family, and this was her real home.

But even as she forgot her old life—first the strongest memories, then the moments between, and then the smallest details of who she was—there was one thought, one memory that never left the recesses of her mind: She'd been happy as a human, happier than she was now underwater. And that tiny thought refused to let Lo fully embrace a lifetime under the waves. She had to at least *look* back to the human world.

Once every deep tide—every fifteen months—the sisters surfaced together. Some to remember, most to remember why they forgot. Why the ocean took the memories of their old lives one grain at a time, the same way the tide pulled the shore out to sea. Why the ocean took their souls. Turned them from humans into...this.

There are lights at the surface. I just need to see them, and I'll never forget what they look like again, Lo told herself. She still felt it was better to remember, to know what she was missing. Most of her sisters had long decided that it was easier to forget.

"Ready?" one of the oldest sisters asked. Her voice was bell-like, musical. All the old ones were beautiful, from their voices to the palms of their hands. They would grow more so every day, until the day they'd float away with the low tide, or maybe in a storm, and never be seen again. They became angels, according to the stories. Most of her sisters believed the angel tale, that old ones went to the surface and were greeted by beautiful men, beautiful women who welcomed them into the sky. Lo had her doubts—most of the girls her age still did, but as they grew old, their doubts faded until they believed steadfastly. She wondered how many days, months, tides this sister had left.

"Is it time?" Lo asked.

"As soon as you feel the tide coming in. Any moment now..."

The old sister paused, waited for the tiniest shift in the ocean, in herself. Changes Lo hadn't noticed when she first arrived, changes she suspected only creatures of the water could appreciate. Lo found the water more marvelous every day, found living in it to be more perfect, more wonderful. . . .

But she still wanted to remember.

The ocean shifted; her sisters rose and slipped upward like a single creature. She followed, the old sister just behind

3

her, waiting for them to call her back, to hold her down to the seafloor like they'd done when she first arrived and fought to break the water's surface for weeks and weeks. But no, it was time. She was several months into her new life; she could be trusted to glimpse the old one. The weight of the water above them grew less and less until...

Lo gasped, dry air filling her lungs. It hurt, but she grinned and forced her eyes open despite the wind. Wind— she remembered wind. Standing in a field near a tiny house, people behind her, her family. When she first arrived at the ocean, she would pick out the most beautiful shells from the ocean floor, send them away in the waves, and hope her family would find them. She would imagine they'd see them, know they were from her, know she was alive... and now, she couldn't remember their faces. She couldn't even remember how many family members she had.

The lights. I need to see the lights, she thought firmly— maybe they'd remind her of her family. She looked up at the stars, the moon, and finally the shore. Two bright lights shone from a spot in the sand, moving along slowly, waving back and forth—

Hands—they were handheld lights, grasped in the palms of humans walking side by side. Walking. *I used to walk*, she thought, but she couldn't stop herself from thinking how ungainly it looked compared with being in the water. She swam forward a little, silent, to get a better look.

A boy and a girl, laughing, talking, the sounds barely audible over the crashing waves. Brilliant-colored lights in

4

pinks, reds, greens, yellows, from the carnival beyond the pier, bounced off their faces—all that light, and yet the two of them somehow looked brighter in comparison. They looked warm. They shone. They looked happy.

"Are you going to try?" one of the sisters asked.

"Him?" Lo answered. "How would I get to him?" The two crossed in front of several houses, then a white building with glowing porch lights, making the couple appear in perfect silhouette.

"You can sing. It works sometimes. And they think we're beautiful. That helps."

"But he has her. He's already in love."

"Maybe you can break it," another sister suggested.

"Don't *you* want to?" Lo answered, looking back at them. This boy's soul, why weren't they fighting over it? They were all older than her, more beautiful, more practiced. Make him love you, kiss him, drown him. Earn his soul, and you get your humanity back—the escape from the ocean that the older girls told her about on her very first day. Yet they were letting her have him, if she wanted.

"Go ahead, Lo," Ry said.

Lo swallowed. She loved her sisters, but she knew—they all knew—they weren't originally meant for the sea. And she wanted to remember her former life completely, return to it, before she became old and beautiful and had forgotten her humanity entirely. *It won't be fair, what will happen to the boy, but it wasn't fair what happened to me, either. That makes it all right, doesn't it?*

5

She couldn't remember what happened to her, what turned her into an ocean girl. It was the strongest memory, the first to go. All Lo remembered was standing at the shore of the ocean with a man whose face she couldn't remember. Her body ached, and there was a jagged wound over her heart. The man sent her into the ocean, told her the other girls would find her. He was one of the angels, Ry told her when she arrived.

Lo doubted that as well.

She touched the scar on her chest, almost faded entirely. There was a voice in her head telling her to stop, to turn back, but she ignored it and swam closer, closer to where the waves crashed against the shore.

Sing, a different voice said. A voice that longed to be human again, the voice of the girl she used to be.

The sisters sang all the time, songs that melded together to form one voice that made the ocean thick with music. Lo opened her lips, let the notes emerge.

The boy stopped first, then the girl. They looked at the ocean. Did they see her? The thought was exhilarating, dangerous. She sang louder; behind her, she heard her sisters join in, voices quiet, guiding her along in the song.

The boy stooped to set his light down in the sand, pointing at the ocean, talking with the girl. He waved at Lo, big arms over his head. He saw her. *He sees me; he's coming for me*—yes, he took tentative steps into the water. *Come, where it's deeper, please....*

The girl yelled, shouted, tried to pull him back, but he took another step, another, another. The song grew louder. Lo extended her hand in the moonlight. He had a handsome face, sharp features like a statue. His clothing, now soaked, clung to his body as he reached toward her.

She took his hand. *Don't be scared*. When he touched her, more memories of her old life slammed into her mind. Being held by her father, the scent of his cologne. The smell of things baking, the way fire leaped up from kindling. She swallowed hard, held on to each memory as long as possible before looking back to the boy's eyes.

"Hello," the boy said. He sounded dazed and blinked furiously. Lo stopped singing, and her sisters' song grew louder in response.

"Do you love me?" Lo whispered.

The boy looked surprised for a moment. Her sisters sang louder—he was having trouble fighting them. "I..." He looked back to the girl on the shore. "I love her. The girl by the church, I love her."

Lo's jaw stiffened; her fingers on the boy's hand tightened. "No, no, you love me."

The ocean shifted again, and some of her sisters stopped singing, started whispering. They were tired of the air touching their skin; they wanted to go back under—they wanted to leave. Lo bit her lip, ran her fingers along the boy's shirt-sleeves. Fabric hanging on a clothesline, laundry being folded, the way towels felt drying off her skin, more memories that proved even harder to hold on to. They skirted out of her mind like little fish, then darted back to the recesses they came from. Forgotten.

By the next deep tide, I'll have forgotten everything, just like them, she thought, glancing back at her sisters. *That's why they didn't want the boy for themselves. They don't care about their souls anymore. I won't care in another fifteen months.*

Now. It has to be now. Be brave. It has to happen.

She pulled the boy closer to her, so that his breath warmed her skin. "Love me."

"I . . ."

There was no time. Maybe he loved her already, maybe that was good enough, maybe—the ocean changed again, and the oldest sisters ducked back underwater. Lo inhaled, grasped both edges of the boy's shirt, pulled him against her lips, and kissed him, pleadingly, sorrowfully, desperately.

Then she pulled the boy under.

He hardly fought at first, still entranced with their song, confused, and she was so much more powerful than him in the water. It was easy to pull him into the deep, down to the ocean floor, so easy that for a minute, Lo was able to forget what she was doing to him. His eyes were growing wider; he began to fight for air, struggle against her. *This is it. It's happening. My soul, I'll go back—*

His eyes rolled back in his head. Lo realized her sisters were everywhere, watching, waiting. She leaned over the boy and kissed him again as the last precious bit of oxygen left his lips and floated to the surface.

And then he was dead.

And nothing else had changed.

Lo stared at her hands, at her feet, waiting for the pale blue color to turn back to shades of peach and pink. Waiting for the urge to surface, to gulp air happily, to swim to the shore and run on the sand.

It didn't come.

"Everyone has to try it for herself," Ry said gently, swimming closer. The boy's body listed on the ocean floor like seaweed. Lo felt sick; she doubled over and hid her head. "We all did. But it never works. You can't make them love you that fast."

"I don't think it's even real, that you can get your soul back," an older girl added. "It's a fairy story. Oh, Lo, don't cry. You have us. You don't need their world now. You don't have to worry about remembering anymore. You can just be happy here. And one day, the angels will come back for you, and it'll be beautiful, Lo. It'll be perfect."

Lo turned and cried into her sisters' arms, for her soul, for the boy, for the memories. Her sisters brushed out her hair and held her close. They pushed the boy's body away so she couldn't see it. They sang songs and began games to take her mind off what had happened.

But when the night ended and her sisters went to sleep, Lo stared at the sun from deep beneath the waves, at the tiny threads of blue light that made their way through the water, down to where she was.

Her soul was gone for good. The boy was dead, the girl left alone on the shore. And for nothing, nothing at all, other than a fairy tale and a few scattered memories of life on land. *Let it go. Let it all go.*

And she allowed herself to forget.

CHAPTER ONE

Celia

My sisters love this place.

It smells like sand and cigarettes and cotton candy, like sunscreen and salt. The scent builds up all summer, and now, at the height of tourist season, it's so thick that I think I could wave an empty bottle around and it would fill with liquid perfume.

We cut through the Skee-Ball parlor and emerge on the main drag of the Pavilion, lights and sounds everywhere, crowds of people with terrible sunburns. My sisters giggle to each other, the two of them perfectly in step ahead of me. We are triplets, but they are the twins, a perfectly matched set with high eyebrows and pretty lips. To most people, we look identical; to one another, my features are a little different. A little off, a not-quite-right replica of Anne and Jane.

"Let's go to the coaster," Anne says, tossing her hair over her shoulders as she looks back at me. "The arcade is dead."

The arcade looks anything but dead, lights and alarms and children weaving between adults' legs, but that's not what she means—she means no guys are there.

We approach the roller coaster, a giant wooden monster that creaks and sways a little every time a car zips along the track. A car at the top of the starter hill pauses. The riders point ahead—the first hill sits snugly against the rickety pier's steps and allows for a spectacular view of the ocean. The riders are watching the waves so intently, so wondrously, that they aren't prepared for the drop. They scream.

I know who my sisters are going to pick before they say it aloud. A group of guys, probably early college or so, leaning on the queue railings. They have tans and are wearing T-shirts that are new but distressed to look old. Jane goes first, brushes by them casually, just enough that her bare arm touches theirs. She smiles, apologizes, and looks to Anne, giving a hardly noticeable tilt of her head. *That one.*

"Hi," Anne says, smiling. She sidles up to the railing, leans over. "Where are you guys from?"

"Raleigh," the target answers, smiling back. "What about you?"

"Here," Anne answers. "We go to Milton's. The boarding school? You pass it when you come in."

"Catholic schoolgirls?" one of the target's friends jokes, making his voice sound fake-sexy, and the others laugh. The target is staring at Anne, though, then Jane, and even lets his eyes flit on me for a moment.

"Not Catholic. Just schoolgirls," Jane says in a way that makes the boys shut up yet entices them at the same time.

"Do you want to get out of here?" Anne says to the target. She leans forward, drums his arm with her fingers. The boy glances at her manicured nails—he knows something is strange about this. But Anne knows exactly what to do. She leans forward, laughs in a way that's less seductive and more girl-next-door.

"Come on. Only the tourists ride this thing," she says to him, teasing the other boys. The target seems to open up a little—he likes the way her voice sounds, you can tell. The way she's pretty and casual and the way she smiles. He thinks she seems fun, interesting.

He doesn't realize they're just using him. Not only for the money he'll spend on us, the compliments he'll throw our way—especially Anne's way. He's just, as Jane puts it, "practice." *How will we know what all we can do with these powers if we don't practice?*

"I can't leave them," the boy says, motioning to his friends.

"Sure you can," Anne says, then, eyes glimmering, teasing, "And you will."

She's right—she's always right. You can't hide your future from Anne.

The powers are our greatest secret. The secret we never told anyone, not even our parents, not even our brothers.

Jane's skill developed first. People called her a perceptive child, but there was much more to it. Then Anne, who knew when I'd fall out of the tree house our brother Lucas made. Mine took longer. I thought maybe I didn't have one, even, when I'd turned seven and still nothing had developed. Anne and Jane pushed me, assured me that mine would be the most impressive of the three of them.

But then it wasn't.

Jane can know a person's present. Anne can know their future. And I can know their past.

Anyone can know a person's past, though. All you have to do is ask them. Anne's and Jane's disappointment was almost palpable, but it was nothing compared with mine. I touch someone, I know what they ate for breakfast yesterday, or what their childhood pet was called—how long ago in the past it was doesn't seem to matter. When I hugged my mother, I knew what she felt like right before her wedding, and that our youngest uncle was secretly her out-of-wedlock first son, yet sometimes I'd hold Anne's hand and see the secret she told Jane twenty minutes before. If I could control what parts of their pasts I see, maybe my power would be useful, maybe I'd think playing with the minds of boys was fun, too—and honestly, I bet I could control it if I practiced the way Anne and Jane do. But I won't risk seeing people's darkest memories just to better play games with my power. It's not worth it.

"Come on," Anne says, laughing. The sound is somehow brighter than all the bells and whistles of the carnival games nearby. "Buy me an ice cream."

"Um…" The boy looks at his friends, who snicker. "Okay."

The boy ducks out of the roller-coaster line and follows us back through the crowd to a stand where a bored-looking girl is dishing out scoops of homemade ice cream. Anne orders, looks expectantly at Jane and me.

"You don't mind, do you?" Anne asks the boy, reaching down to touch his arm—skin on skin, that's all it takes for our powers to work. She flashes a smile, tilts her head, all the things that she knows the boy wants, if only because at that angle he can see down her shirt a little. He doesn't mind. They rarely mind, even if it's dinner or movie tickets or letting Jane drive their fancy sports cars. I think that's Anne's favorite part: She knows just what to do and say to make them not care.

The boy buys us ice cream, banana-pudding-flavored, and then pays for a few rounds at the arcade. Jane finally shakes her head, though—he's starting to think less of us, to suspect we're just using him. So we drop him like a broken toy, sending him back to his friends pissed off that the antici- pated hookup isn't happening. We don't care. After all, he was just practice.

I don't really know what we're practicing for, nor do I know how scamming boys out of money helps us understand our powers. I don't think Anne and Jane know, either—they just like playing the game and want to justify it. They like being in control. Their powers give them that.

All my power does is weigh me down with everyone's sorrow, everyone's tragedies, things that can't be changed or

15

altered or fixed. It makes me afraid to talk to people for too long, worried I'll reveal things about them I know yet shouldn't know. It's easier just to keep everyone away. Never touch them. Never read them.

My sisters' powers are gifts. My power is a curse.

The three of us crash onto a bench in front of the Haunted Hotel ride, where rickety cars squeal through a darkened building. The drunker the tourists get, the more they love it, even though it smells like a basement and the fake corpses have twenty years of dust on them.

"This is boring," Jane sighs. "All the good ones were here earlier in the season."

"We could go home and watch that movie," I suggest.

"Ugh, no, it's Friday night! What about him?" Jane says, pointing to a handsome guy who's holding a girl's hand, in line to ride the carousel.

"He's with *her*," Anne answers.

"Yeah…" Jane sighs. Their rule is, they don't use their powers to trick boys who are in love. Maybe it's too many romantic comedies and sappy novels, maybe it makes them feel like what they do is perfectly okay, but they've held their ground on that one, Anne more easily than Jane.

Anne begins to roll her eyes, but before she's finished, Jane reaches over and grabs her hand. Anne yanks it away, irritated.

"Don't do that!" she snaps. We don't use our powers on one another, and thus we try to avoid touching—but it's a rule Jane has always found more flexible than Anne or me.

"Come on, it's easier than wandering around all night. What did you see?" Jane asks.

Anne glares at her for a moment but finally reveals what she saw in Jane's future. "There's a tall guy somewhere, green shirt, I think. He'll take us to that fondue place, if you want to go."

"I hate that place," I say, and the truth is, I think Anne and Jane do, too—they just like that it's expensive. I'd be happier with a three-dollar hot dog from the street vendor.

"*Everyone* loves that place," Anne argues. "Come on, let's find him."

"I'll catch up later," I say. Anne and Jane look at me, then each other, like I'm turning up my nose at an amazing adventure. When we were little, we were interlocked, like the three strands of a braid—pull one, and the others fall apart. But now, even though Anne is always reminding me that "we're stronger together," I can't help but feel differently. They're stronger without me. Sure, maybe I'm weak, maybe I'm nothing without them, but to be honest, I'm pretty sure I'm nothing with them, too.

"Fine," Anne sighs. "We'll see you at home, I guess."

I'll give it to my sisters—they *want* me to be one of them. The third piece to their matching set. But wanting is not enough, so while they wander off in search of a target in green, I weave through a row of food carts and toward the coaster, toward the pier.

The pier juts off a short cliff and is eerily dark compared with the Pavilion—its old lights can't conquer the enormous blackness of both the sky and the nighttime ocean. A few lovers look out over the sea, a guitarist with an open case for tips sings a song I don't recognize, and a handful of fishermen tend to their lines. I look down at the water. The tide is massive tonight, the perigean tide, if my memories from astronomy class are correct. As I go farther and farther toward the pier's end, the sound of the Pavilion fades, replaced by the powerful noise of the ocean.

We're from the middle of Georgia, a tiny landlocked town and a house full of siblings—all brothers, save me, Anne, and Jane. It doesn't make sense that I feel most myself when I'm alone by the ocean. Maybe it's because I think the ocean is like me. It knows the past. It's seen yachts and ships and pirates and a time before people. It has secrets, secrets you don't know just by watching the surface.

I look down the beach, which is illuminated only by moonlight and the glow of the Pavilion. This isn't a swimming section—it's too rocky. Most of the houses at the bottom of the little cliff, right on the sea, were abandoned a year or so ago when a hurricane battered them beyond repair. There's an old church, a single-room building with faded graffiti—cheap spray paint doesn't last long against the ocean's spray, so it looks like the church has a pastel hue.

The guitar player wanders near me, still playing and singing under his breath. He's wearing a shirt that's real vintage—it has a few tiny holes, and the sleeves are stretched out. I can't tell if he's handsome or not, but I want to keep looking at his face, thin lips and deep-set eyes. I don't have any money

18

and hate to give him false hope for tips, so I turn away, back to the water. I wonder how deep it is. I wonder how deep it is everywhere.

The guitarist stops playing, I hear something like running or stomping. I turn around, eyebrows raised, just in time to see it happen.

He trips on an uneven plank. He tries to catch himself but throws his weight backward to keep from falling forward on the guitar. Everyone is watching, no one is moving. It happens so fast—he's off balance, hits the railing of the pier at just the right angle. The right angle to fall into the blackness, into the ocean.

CHAPTER TWO

Lo

We don't want to go to the surface.
We linger under the water, down deep, where it's cold; it makes us feel the most alive. Only the new girl wants to go up. Her skin is still a little pink, like it remembers the sun, whereas most of ours are pale, with places tinted the light purples, blues, or greens of seashells.

It's nice that we look the same, that we are the same. It means we are safe, because there are dozens and dozens of me. When they move, I move; when I move, they move. It has long stopped surprising me, the speed at which new girls forget their first names. You don't need a name when everyone is you and you are everyone.

I'm still on my second name, Lo, the sound the water makes during a thunderstorm when you're deep beneath the waves. But eventually, I'll forget this one, too. I'll move on to a third, maybe even a fourth, until I'll give up on names altogether, like the oldest of us have.

The pull of the tide gets stronger; the full moon is rising. The new girl looks up through the softened wooden planks of the *Glasgow*'s deck, and the tiny bit of moonlight streaking to the depths illuminates her face. She looks sweet, kind, gentle. Human. She lifts, releases the rock she was holding on to, and starts toward the surface.

"I suppose it's time," Key says, lingering just outside the cracked ship's hull. She and I came to the ocean just a few months apart. Her name used to be Julia. I don't know why I can remember her old name but not my own. Key sighs and pushes off the ocean floor; sand blossoms around her bare feet as she swims upward. She never wants to surface. Whatever happened in her human life, she was more than happy to forget it long ago—I don't think she even tried to remember, to be honest.

But nonetheless, she'll still surface—we all will, because we are the same thing. My hair floats around my body like a cloak, then trails along behind me as I kick off the ground, dodge the caved-in bits of the ship. I follow Key, faster, faster; I can feel the others behind me as the *Glasgow* fades from sight. The water cradles us from every direction until we break the surface, and I feel so, so . . .

Exposed. Like I'm falling into the sky. The air hurts my skin, and I close my eyes to the pain. Around me, I hear the gentle splash of the others breaking the surface, winces or gasps as they remember what the shore looks like. I brace myself and open my eyes.

Light, so much light—from the moon, from the tiny pin-prick stars, but mostly from the pier and the city beyond. It glows; it's beautiful in a way that nothing beneath the water is. I inhale even though it burns, brush a few strands of dark hair from my face.

The new girl—Molly, her name is Molly, I think—has tears running down her cheeks—they're somehow so different from the ocean water, so unusual that I notice them immediately.

"You won't miss it as much, eventually," Key reassures her. It's true—I don't miss my old life at all. I don't remember it, of course, but even if I did, I'm happy here. I have my sisters, the ocean. . . .

"I don't want to stop missing it," the girl says. The words were clearly supposed to be sharp, but they're softened by her crying.

"Well," someone else says, "find your mortal boy, then."

A few girls chuckle, but inside we all feel the same twinge of pity for her hope. It's the cruelest thing, hope, the way it strings you along, the way it makes you believe. Only the old ones have ever seen a mortal's soul stolen, and they can barely remember it to tell us the story. They say she walked, though—she walked right out of the sea; her skin was pink again, her lungs made for air instead of water.

It's *hard* to believe sometimes, but hope never lets you truly stop believing. Our souls fade slowly, just like our human memories—I imagine mine is gone entirely now, though to be honest, I'm not sure. What does having a soul feel like, exactly? I still believe that drowning a human would get me a new soul, but it's not something I care to pursue anymore, and I'm somewhat relieved to feel that way, especially when I look at the tortured, desperate look on Molly's face. She must still feel her soul, feel it bleeding out of her. That's the only explanation for the pain in her eyes.

Music, we hear music bouncing across the water and audible only in the seconds between waves lapping at our shoulders. A light and airy song, and then beyond that, the buzz of a crowd. How many people are there that we can hear them from this far away?

I look at Key, at the others. They stare, either at the moon, the pier, or the tiny little houses on the shore. Do people still live in them? They look different than when I saw them last, more chipped and faded, like the ocean has punished them. I wonder where the people who lived there went. Someplace far away from the water?

I don't even know what that sort of place would look like, I think, shivering a little.

There's a bang somewhere ahead, a shout. It's coming from the pier—we stare as a dark form falls over its railing, into the water. There's a horrible slapping sound when the thing hits, splashing, screams from those above.

We are silent. We don't move, staring, like one creature with dozens of heads, dozens of eyes watching curiously. We see a thousand times better than we did as humans, but the waves block our line of sight. Then, in one motion, we dive forward, slipping through the water toward the pier.

It's splashing—*he's* splashing desperately. The waves are unusually harsh tonight, and his clothes weigh him down.

We watch. Oldest in the back, apathetic, here only because the rest of us are. Youngest closest to him, intrigued, wondering how long before he'll slip under the water and die. Me, somewhere between the two groups. It's so strange to watch the boy struggle, fight against something that's so natural for us.

But the new girl is watching with a different sort of intensity than the rest of us. She inhales, draws closer to him. She's shaking; he's thrashing, trying to swim, but every time he gets his head up, a wave knocks him down again. There's something strapped around his shoulders that's pulling him beneath. The new girl turns back to look at us as the boy's flails slow; he begins to go under more often....

"How do I make him love me?" the new girl asks.

"That's the tricky part," Key says, eyes flickering like this is a brilliant game—most things are to her. "It's hard to make someone love you when they're dying."

Key's words seem to both scare and embolden the new girl. She presses her lips together hard, sinks under the water, and emerges beside the boy. He grabs hold of her arm to try to keep his head up. It works; he stops fighting the waves, but when he breathes, I can hear the water in his lungs.

"My name is Molly," the new girl says. He doesn't hear her, but her voice is delicate, rainlike. The boy turns his shaky eyes toward her, but I don't think he really sees her face—he looks unfocused, dazed.

"Yes, there, see," Molly says, grinning so wide the moonlight glints off her teeth. His eyes begin to drift shut. She shakes him awake, says her name again, tries to talk to him. When it doesn't work, she begins to sing. Her voice is pure, lovely, just enough humanity in it to remind me how she was a human girl less than a year ago. The song is one of ours, but it seems foreign on her tongue.

I look away from her, toward the pier the boy came from. People stare in our direction, but they can't see us in the darkness. But then there's a rustle from the shore, and something comes down the road by the beaten-looking buildings, bright flashing red lights that bounce across the water.

"They're coming for him," one of the girls says. Molly stops singing, looks up.

"Leave him," another girl tells Molly. "There's no time. And no point."

"There's time—there has to be time," Molly says, voice rough and dangerous. She positions herself in front of the boy's face, water dripping off her eyelashes. His eyes drift shut. "No, look at me. Look at me. Do you love me?"

"It's too fast," I tell her, grimacing as a breeze touches my shoulders. I lean back so they're wet again.

"Was it like this for the other girl? Or did it take longer?" Key asks one of the oldest ones; she doesn't answer. Key shrugs. "I remember human stories about love at first sight."

"Those were *stories*," I say. Lights, bright white and big

like the moon, shine at the waves from the shore farther down the beach. They're making their way toward us, rolling steadily along. We can't stay. We don't want them to see us. We don't want to see humans, really; the oldest girls are finding it difficult to even look at the human boy, his head cradled against Molly's shoulder.

There's a quiet sound, like raindrops—we're leaving. My sisters slip underneath the water delicately, more and more with every moment. When I look back to Molly, the boy's eyes are open again. They aren't trained on her, though—he's looking at us—no, at *me*, I think. Not in the dizzy, confused way he was watching Molly earlier, but like he knows me, like we're in the middle of a conversation. His eyes are light gray pools that remind me of the ice that forms by the ocean farther north. His gaze startles me, and I back up, my lips part.

"Go with them if you want. I'm not leaving till he says he loves me," Molly sniffs. She's crying, so humanlike that she and the boy actually seem a perfect match. She looks down at the boy's face and follows his gaze to me. She frowns and turns him around, so he can't see me. I swallow hard; it feels like his eyes are still boring into me. I realize that in the long moment of the boy's gaze, my sisters have left. I'm alone with Molly.

"Leave him. He doesn't need to die like this. He doesn't love you."

"He might!"

"No, Molly," I say, and grimace as I remember the boy I killed. The way his body rocked with the currents, dead and

26

lifeless on the floor. I don't want to imagine the boy with the gray eyes like that. Hope forces me to believe getting his soul is possible—I don't know *how*, exactly, but I believe it's possible—but something deeper makes me believe it isn't right. And it certainly isn't right like this, when I know there's no chance Molly will walk out of the ocean tonight.

Yet I know what Molly feels. I may not remember my human name like she does, but I remember being her. I remember needing to believe the fairy tale, in thinking of hope as a real thing instead of a pretty idea. I swim closer to her.

"Let him go," I say, trying to sound gentle, comforting. "His people will find him. We need to leave. We don't belong here." I feel unsettled without the others on the surface, like I've lost a part of myself.

Molly's fingers are wrapped so tightly around him that I can see his skin starting to bruise. The lights on the beach are moving, growing closer, little by little. A puttering noise bounces toward us—a boat coming from somewhere, probably more searchers. The thing weighing the boy down brushes against my legs, the strings sharp like sea urchin spines, some sort of instrument, I think.

I reach forward and take Molly's arm, try to pull her away. She struggles, hugs the boy against her chest like she suspects I'm trying to steal him from her. I find myself wishing he'd look at me again, fighting Molly harder and harder, trying to get her away from him.

Molly dives.

Still holding the boy.

Let her go. We all have to try this for ourselves once. It's the only way Molly will stop fighting and embrace the ocean, embrace our sisters. She needs to kill the boy to love the ocean the way we do.

But the boy's eyes, I keep thinking about the boy's eyes. He doesn't need to die like this.

I sink into the water and swim after her. She's swimming fast, pulling him to the bottom with such force that the instrument comes loose and drifts to the ocean floor on its own.

"Molly!" I call out. "Let him go! There's no point! You'll just kill him!"

"That's what I'm supposed to do—that's how I'll get my soul back!" she snarls. We're getting deeper, to the part where it's cold. The boy's limbs flail back uselessly. His eyes are closed; he's not even fighting. I think he's already dead.

Molly slams his head against the sea bottom, frustrated; a little blood curls like smoke in the water. His clothes and hair float around his body as she bows her head and presses her lips against his. Nothing happens, nothing changes, and so she tries again, again, until it looks less like a kiss and more like she's trying to pull his soul up and out through his lips.

She screams, a curdling, agonizing sound that ripples through the ocean. Molly tightens her fingers on the boy's clothes—

Enough. I dart forward and grab his arm, yank him away

from her. Molly hisses at me, grabs at his sleeve. His shirt rips, but I'm older and stronger than she is. I jettison him to the surface, hold his head up as the air tastes my skin. There has to be a boat nearby now. They'll find him; they'll take him back to his own kind, and I can go back to mine. *That's the way of things; it's what should happen.* He's so limp that he feels fake, like he's a clump of seaweed instead of a boy.

Molly breaks out of the water beside me, I release him just long enough to shove her away. Her teeth flicker, sharp like an animal's. Where's the boat?

They've passed us. They're searching farther from the pier now; I can't get him there with Molly like this. The shore, it's the only way. Get him close enough, and the waves will wash him up, someone will find him, he might survive. Molly tries to pull me back; I dodge her and kick her in the back. She spirals off in the water. I'll have just a moment before she slows herself and returns. I clutch the boy under the arms and drag him toward the dry sand.

The waves help, pushing us over the sandbar—closer to land than I've been since I joined my sisters. But there's someone on the shore; he'll be found. I hiss in Molly's direction and grab the boy's wrist, diving forward, letting the waves throw me closer and closer to the shore with each step. The person on the beach sees me. A girl, running. *Take him. Take him and keep him away from us.*

Shallow water. I turn back to look for Molly—she's stopped, waiting for me right where the water becomes deep again, where the waves begin. The girl runs into the water, awkward and clumsy as it splashes around her calves. There's not enough force behind the waves to pull him forward here. My feet find the sandy bottom, and I rise—

Something stings, something hurts. We haven't walked on land in so long; did it always feel like this? One step forward, another, another, it feels like something is sticking into the center of my foot. Never mind, the salt water will heal it fast enough. Just get him to her; then I can leave....

She's near me now, breathing heavily, hair stuck to her cheeks and chest. She smells strange, but I'm not sure what the scent is, exactly—the scent of land? She grabs one of the boy's arms, and I release him, move to dive back into the ocean. I want to be submerged. I want to go back down deep where it's cold.

The girl slows. She moves clumsily in the water; without help, she can barely even drag the boy. A small wave rocks her balance, and she's forced to drop a knee into the sand to keep from falling.

"Help me!" she says, sounding irritated. Her voice is biting and loud—this whole world is biting and loud. I grimace and take his other arm, rise again, wincing as something stabs at my sole.

Together, we drag the boy through the last of the waves. As the water grows shallower, the pain gets worse. Something is stabbing me, slicing at my feet, at the softest parts of my toes and the center of my arch. I have to stop, I have to stop walking. I'm not meant for this anymore, but we're almost out, almost out, almost...

We reach the edge of the water. As the wave pulls back, my foot strikes damp sand.

The pain is incredible. I fall to my knees, then my hands, dropping the boy's arms so I can grab my foot. There's blood, blood everywhere, like the entire bottom of my foot has been scraped away. I try to find the wound, but it's dark.

"Do you know CPR?" the girl asks.

"What?"

"CPR?"

I stare at her. She looks frustrated but then pauses for a moment. Her eyes drop to my chest.

"You're naked."

She's right. My sisters and I, we're all naked, aren't we? It's never bothered us. Maybe I should cover myself, but between the searing pain in my feet and the dying boy at my side, it doesn't seem to matter very much.

"Right, CPR," the girl says, shaking her head. Her hair is blond and thick like sea grass. She tips the boy onto his back, puts her palms on his chest, then begins pressing it. Quick, tiny pushes, over and over. She leans down near his lips and listens, puts her lips over his for an instant, repeats. The girl jumps back, puts a hand to her lips as though he's shocked her, but nothing changes with the boy. She looks at me desperately, like she wants me to step in, but I don't understand what she's doing.

"I... I can't do it, I—*Help! He's down here!*" she shouts to the people farther down the beach, to the flashing red lights. I don't think they hear her. I listen to the water, wait for it to tell me that a long wave is washing up—that's all I'll need to pull myself back in without standing, without the pain. I don't care if the human girl sees me. I want to go home. Blood from my feet has stained the sand. It hurts, it hurts so badly.

"You can do compressions," the girl says suddenly. I look at her blankly. "Compressions! You can do them. Come on, at least try."

She reaches over the boy and grabs my arm, starts to pull it to the boy's chest—

She freezes. So do I.

When was the last time a human touched me? I stare at her fingers wrapped around my skin, bright on the gray-blue hue of my forearm. Her palm is so hot—or am I just that cold? The girl gasps, yanks her hand away. She looks me in the eye like I've betrayed her, like I've done or said something unforgivable, something shocking.

Her words are whispered, hardly audible over the sound of waves.

"Naida."

I . . .

I know that name.

Naida. I turn it over in my mind. I know that name. How did she know it?

That's my name. Not Lo, I'm Naida. Or I was.

I remember. I remember having a flesh-and-blood sister, not ocean sisters. I remember a house, I remember warm meals, I remember the sound of crickets and what the world looks like miles and miles from the shore.

My name on her lips echoes through my head, spins around me, and deafens me to the rest of the world, dulls the pain in my feet. *My name is Naida, and I was once a human girl.*

I remember.

I remember everything. I remember my house, my real sister, my father, our dog, bedtime stories, running in the grass. I remember riding in cars and dancing and the way rainstorms sounded when they passed through the forest we lived in.

I remember being Naida. I remember being human. But only for a moment, and then the memories begin to fade, fall apart. The harder I try to hold on, the more they slip through my fingers like grains of sand.

The boy coughs, sputters. Water bubbles up from his throat. The girl turns his head to the side. His eyes open; he tries to focus as he looks at me—it makes my chest stir, makes me forget the pain, to see his gray eyes open again. His gaze turns to the girl. He's confused. But he's alive. He's alive— that's all I wanted. I can go. My sisters are in the water; they're my world now. I can't be Naida, not anymore. I killed my boy; I embraced the ocean long ago.

"You saved him," the girl says breathlessly, like she can't believe it. She looks back up at me, but I'm already on my feet.

I cry out in pain as I run back into the water, every step like knives twisting into my skin, pain that doesn't stop until I dive deep. But as I do so, I chant the name over and over in my head, so I won't ever forget it again.

Naida.

CHAPTER THREE

✖

Celia

She's gone.

She's in the water. I don't know what to do—it's so dark out there, I wouldn't be able to see myself, much less find her. I look down at the footprints she left in the sand as she ran back toward the water, lit up by the moon. They're darker than they should be. I kneel down and touch the center of a print. Blood. It's blood.

A wave sweeps high across the shore, dragging the footprint into long, misshapen lines, and then another that washes away all traces of the blood. I squeeze my eyes shut— I feel dizzy. I saw the girl's past, and just before that, the boy's. My head feels crowded, like my own thoughts can't breathe under the weight of their memories—especially hers. Her memories were wrong; they were darkened, like someone painted black over them. My head aches....

The boy coughs. I turn around, drop back to the sand

beside him. His eyes are closed, but he's breathing, a broken noise, like there's wet cloth lodged in his throat. The ambulance is rumbling down the tiny road by the pier, the same way I came down. The headlights blind me as it draws close.

"Hang on," I tell the boy. "You're fine. They're here to help you."

He whispers something, something quiet. I lean closer, drop my face near his lips. "Sing again."

He's confused. Of course, I just saw a naked girl with bloody feet run into the ocean, so perhaps I'm not one to talk. The ambulance reaches us, slides to a stop on the sand. I sit back as the paramedics leap out. They run to us, drop down by my side, start talking in codes I don't understand. I'm jostled out of the way as they lift his body, then rest it down on a board. One paramedic, a younger woman with thin eyes, spots me as two men lift the board and hurry the boy to the ambulance.

"Was he breathing when you found him?"

"Yes. I mean no, no. He started, though."

"Any idea how long he was in the water?"

"I . . . four minutes? Five? I don't know. It all happened so fast. When I ran down here, she was already pulling him up. . . ." I glance back at the pier. A crowd has gathered, pointing at us, gaping.

"She? Is there someone else here?" the woman asks, looking around.

I swallow, look out over the water. The red lights from the ambulance bounce off the waves, like thousands of glistening rubies are hiding under them. "No. There's no one else here." It's not entirely a lie—she's gone. I can't explain who she is or where she went to myself, much less to someone else.

"Is she coming?" another paramedic yells.

"Can we take you to the hospital, miss? You might need to get checked out, too," the woman says, taking a few steps backward, toward the ambulance. "Come on, it won't take long. Just in case."

"Yes. Yes, right," I say hurriedly. I'm fine; I know I'm fine, but I want to know the boy will be okay—and I don't want to be left out here in the dark, not with the crowd staring, not with a mysterious girl who might come back. I jog with the woman to the ambulance. A male paramedic stretches out a large hand to help me in. I'm quickly moved toward the back, near the boy's head. There's a mask over his nose and mouth, bags of fluids are on hooks, things are beeping, moving. It feels like I'm a giant in a city of machines. I bang my elbow on something behind me, grimace, and try to catch my breath.

"Do you know who he is?" an EMT asks me.

"Jude," I say quickly. I look up. "His name is Jude Wallace. He's from Lake City."

"Oh, so you actually know him. I'm sorry—I thought you were just a good Samaritan," the EMT says, smiling at me. I don't know what to do, so I just nod. Truth is, I *do* know him, and rather well. When I put my lips against his to save his life, I saw deeper into his past than I've ever seen into anyone's before. I saw his childhood home, his father leaving, his first job, second job, third job, and the bank account he opened to save up and leave town when he graduated from high school. I saw his first love and his favorite color, thousands of bits and pieces, a kaleidoscope of his life.

It's the first time my lips have been on someone else's. Does that count as my first kiss? I'd avoided it for so long, both because most boys want Anne and Jane, but also because of this. Anne and Jane have always said kissing makes their powers strong, that the more intimate the touch, the closer you are, the more you can see. They were telling the truth, it seems.

The ambulance screeches through town, the siren blending in seamlessly with the fanfare of the beach at summer. They've stopped working on Jude, and his breathing doesn't sound painful anymore. The hospital is just outside town, where there are no tourists, no neons, no bathing suits—just sea grass and trailer parks. I watch them fly by, look out the window hoping to see the glow of the hospital's fluorescent lights ahead....

"You can hold his hand if you want," the thin-eyed woman says when she sees me staring at him.

"No," I answer. "It's fine." I want to take his hand, to be honest—I don't want him to be scared. I want him to know someone is there with him, someone is thinking of him, someone wants him to survive. But I've already seen so far into his mind, and I don't want to pry any further.

We arrive, and the boy is rushed off the ambulance and

down a hall. They send me to a separate room, but it doesn't take more than a half hour for them to realize I'm fine. A woman in cat-print scrubs gives me a package of Nutter Butters, then leads me toward a waiting room. She talks the entire time, assuring me that everything will be all right with Jude, that they'll update me soon, that they will let me know the minute he wakes up. All well-rehearsed lines, delivered with sincerity, but not enough to distract me from the onslaught of Jude's memories and the strangeness of Naida's.

I load sugar into a cup of weak tea from a machine and rest in one of the many uncomfortable chairs, trying to tune out the noise from the televisions, the people talking in the hallways. Tune them all out and remember...

I ran down to the shore, past the church. I could see someone in the water. I thought it was the boy, but no...it was her. She was swimming toward me, toward the shore. I remember her face, try to imagine what it would look like in the day instead of illuminated by blue moonlight. I picture the way she slipped into the ocean like the waves were sheets on a bed when she left, and the way she rose from the water when she arrived, pulling Jude like the waves worked with her, not against her. The memories I read when I touched her arm. So strange...Even once I got past the blackness, the memories I saw were like memories of a past lifetime instead of the current one. Bits and pieces, buried so deep that all I got from touching her was her name and the memory of a girl screaming.

Screaming like she was dying.

I play the memory over and over, think about the bloody footprints, the way she vanished. Should I have told them about her? Is it too late now? Should I go back?

An hour later, I still have no idea what happened on the beach.

"He's going to wake up soon. You can wait, if you want. Is he your boyfriend?" the doctor asks.

I blush before I can stop myself. "No," I say, shaking my head. "I don't know him."

"Oh? They said—"

"They misunderstood. I just know his name; he told me before he passed out on the beach," I explain swiftly. Now that I'm a little calmer, I can lie better.

"Ah. So you went into the ocean to pull a complete stranger out of the water? What a hero," the doctor says genuinely, putting a hand on my shoulder.

"Thank you," I answer, and force a smile. *No, I didn't go into the water. I stayed on the shore while Naida pulled him out. She's the one who really saved him.*

"Well, feel free to stay if you want. I'm sure he'd like to meet you," the doctor says. He tucks his clipboard under his arm and walks away, leaving me alone in the waiting room. The television goes to a commercial, something about a magically absorbent towel. Outside, a pack of nurses laugh loudly. I would like to meet him, too—the real way, not the way I already have.

But I'm afraid he'll ask about Naida. I'm afraid he'll know I'm lying, that I didn't really save him, not alone, anyway. I'm afraid of how much I know about him—even worse, how I *liked* so many of the things I saw, like his middle school talent-show performance or the way he worried about asking his first girlfriend to prom. And I'm afraid I won't be able to hide the sheer quantity of memories I read. It'd be easier to walk away, to keep him at arm's length. He's just a boy, just like any of the boys Anne and Jane pick up. Just leave him here.

It'd be better for everyone if I just went home.

CHAPTER FOUR

Lo

"You stole him!" Molly screams at me. Bubbles slip from her lips; her eyes are red, her hands clenched in fists. "He was mine!" Her voice is like lightning caught in the walls of the *Glasgow*. Fish dart away as she grabs onto a decaying stair rail so hard that it rips away from the spiral banister. She drops it and screams again. I've never seen one of us so angry before. The other girls try to comfort her, save the old ones, who regard her with mild curiosity from just outside the ship's body, like she's nothing more than an interesting bit of coral or a strange tide.

"He didn't love you. There was no need to kill him." I try to sound calm, even-keeled, like Molly is nothing more than an insolent child. But I'm shaken; I feel like I could dissolve into the water around me.

The girl. The girl on the shore knew my name. Naida.

While Molly curses at me, I turn the name over in my

mind. The memories it sparked when I first heard it are dull, faded now, and I'm having trouble bringing them up. But the name, the name I can remember if I just keep repeating it. I don't know why I care. Naida is long gone. And yet over and over, I keep saying it, don't let go—

"Do you, Lo?" Key asks.

"I..." I look at Key, who draws closer to me. We look so different than humans, don't we? I'd forgotten till I saw the girl, but now, compared with Key...you would never know we were once like them. What did my hair look like when I was Naida? What color was my skin? I look down at my arm, at the milky-blue color. Key's is milky-green. But when we were humans, we must have been bronze or golden or some sun-kissed color. I haven't thought about these things in ages, yet now I stare at my forearm in wonder, in sorrow that I can't remember what it once looked like. Who can't remember her own body?

"I was telling her that you didn't want the boy's soul any-how? You sound like one of the old ones, Lo. Should I hold on to you if a hurricane passes through?" Her words are teas-ing, but the humor doesn't reach her eyes. I do sound like one of the old ones—they don't listen. They don't care. They're as quiet as the sand, letting the water push them around like branches of seaweed. Getting their attention is hard.

But I don't feel old. I feel like I did when I was new, when I was younger than Molly, even. *Naida. Naida. I can't forget it again. Naida.*

They're staring at me, waiting for me to answer. "No.

43

No, I didn't want his soul. I just see no point in needless death," I say, waving my hand in Molly's direction. It's not a lie. I don't care about the boy—I liked his eyes, the way he looked at me, but right now I care about my name. I care about how a human girl knew my name.... Did I know her when I was like them? *Please, Molly, let it go. I just want to focus on my name—*

Naida.

"He might have loved me. It might have worked," Molly hisses. Her hair is red—or, it was red. It's now faded and darkened by the sea. Still, it's the most vibrant hair among us, and it blossoms around her face. It never mattered to me before, but now I scan my sisters, picking out the differences, the tiny differences between us. Darker skin, longer torsos, fuller lips. Only the old ones look the same, like the ocean beat their differences out of them, made them all equally beautiful. I'll look like that eventually. And so will Molly. I look back at her, suddenly envious that her hair is still so red. I notice calluses on each of her left fingers. What did she do as a human to earn those?

"I'm sorry," I tell her, drawing closer. "I didn't mean it. Forgive me." When a sister asks forgiveness, there's really little choice. We have to forgive one another, the old ones say, because none of us can get by alone. We don't lie to one another, we don't hold grudges, we don't hate. It wouldn't make any sense to.

"It was my one chance. My only chance to escape. I could

have gone back! I could have fought, could have gotten revenge for what happened to us...." Her words are mournful, but her face is not. I raise my eyebrows—I don't understand what she means by revenge, and from my sisters' confused expressions, neither do they. It's something we've forgotten, and it's hard to care about things you've forgotten, I suppose. Molly sees this and exhales, shakes her head like we're too stupid to understand. Just as I'm about to ask her to explain, she swims closer to me, and the water around her feels hot. I watch, waiting, wondering if she's too young to understand forgiveness. Was I ever this young?

"Forgive me," I repeat. Molly stares at me for a long time. Her eyes flicker, pools within the ocean that seem so shallow, yet so dangerous.

"It's a good thing, Molly," one of the other girls says. "It wouldn't have worked anyhow, and now you can be happy with us. Your sisters."

"Exactly," I say, voice unconvincing—last night I would have been able to persuade her, to tell her how beautiful it is under the water when a storm passes overhead, how perfect we all are together. Those things are still true, and yet... I try to shake off the sense of longing, a sharp pain that strikes at my chest.

Molly hisses at me, and for a tiny, tiny moment, I think she's going to attack. She'll lose—I'm older, stronger. She seems to realize this; she pulls backward like the water itself is sucking her away. Molly folds her arms across her waist

45

as if she's sick, swims up the ship's staircase, probably headed to one of the few bedrooms on the upper floor. When I was new, I spent ages sequestered in the back of the largest bedroom, lingering by a sunken-in bed, trying to pretend everything was normal, that this was a normal room in a house on land. I stared at the coral-covered globe, tried to close the curtains—they disintegrated like dead seaweed in my hands. I wish I could help Molly, wish I could tell her that I understand, but that I just couldn't let her—

"You *should* have let her have him," one of my sisters says, our thoughts as matched as our bodies.

"It would have been easier," another echoes. "Now she won't realize that it can never work."

"She'll understand eventually," I answer. "She'll learn to be happy here. We all did."

Key smiles at me. Her teeth glisten, too sharp compared with the human girl's. "True, but you had to kill your boy to understand. Now she'll always wonder."

I grimace as I remember the boy I killed. That's one thing that hasn't faded over time—the memory of his limp body, of pressing my cheek against his chest and realizing his lungs were full of water, not air. Key is right, though; I know she is. I had to try, had to know that getting a soul wasn't as simple as singing a boy close to you. No wonder Molly can't really forgive me.

The crowd of my sisters disperses, somewhat. They split off into groups to braid one another's hair, lie in the sand, race around the *Glasgow* until they collapse into fits of laughter. The old ones sit on the ship's deck, occasionally looking up when the new ones zip past but mostly staring endlessly into the sea. It's like they see something we don't, deep in the ocean. Like they're waiting for something they're certain is coming. For the angels to come back for them. Did the angel who brought me here know who I used to be? Did he know what happened to me? Did he know—

My name. My name, my human name. I had it, moments ago, but...My throat feels tight, my stomach twisted. It's gone; it can't be gone. I can't lose it again. Remember, remember, I have to remember—

Naida.

I exhale in relief. I still have it. I haven't lost it. I lie back in the sand, dig my toes into it, and close my eyes. If I stare straight up, I can see the light of the moon. The water distorts it, throws it around with each wave that passes overhead. *Naida.*

I wonder what Naida was like when she came to the sea. I wonder where she was from. Molly was from New York. She wanted to be a singer. I remember those details about her because she cried them to us over and over, all the plans she had for her human life that now had to be forgotten. There was more, I'm sure, but I don't remember them, and I doubt Molly does, either. We all forget when we come to the ocean.

An old one told me once that we weren't brought to the ocean because we are ocean girls—we came to the ocean because we were trying to cling to our humanity. She said when we changed, we started to slip, fall away from our human selves, and the angel, he knew the ocean could remind us what being human felt like. It is beautiful, it is endless, it is full and yet seems empty. It hurts us. It tosses us around, rakes our backs across rocks, stings our eyes with sand and salt water. The ocean makes us feel everything and, for a little while, makes us feel human again, until finally even the water isn't strong enough to keep our humanity from slipping away. We become sea creatures, because only the sea loves us, and we give up the silly idea of our humanity.

Yet the girl on the shore, she knew my name. Did I know her? Were we friends, so close that she could recognize me even now? I try to remember her face, place it in my old life, but my mind won't allow me to hold on to my name and the girl's face. I let her image slide away. The name is more important. I don't know why—I'm Lo now, and I'm happy. I'm happy here, right now, in this moment. I don't need to remember Naida, to fight for memories that are as decayed as the *Glasgow*.

But ... I close my eyes, say the name again.

Should I tell the others about the girl on the beach? About how my feet bled when I stepped in the sand? Most of us wouldn't care, I'm sure. Molly might. The others would be disappointed that I spoke with a human; unless we're after their souls, it's best they don't see us. I don't like having a secret, though. Secrets make me different. Secrets make me alone, make me unhappy.

But I decide not to tell them. I close my eyes, let the waves swish my hair up and over my body until the moon drops low and the ocean gets dark, so dark that I know it's nearly dawn. All the while I repeat the name in my head—no, not *the* name. My name.

Naida. Naida. Naida.

CHAPTER FIVE

❧

Celia

I take a cab from the hospital back to our dorm. The campus is dark, but it always is during the summer—the old, weather-beaten brick buildings loom like monsters amid the palm trees. The upper dormitories, where my sisters and I live, are the most lonesome of all. Most of the girls who go to Milton's Prep come from money and spend their summers on islands or yachts or in foreign countries. They return in August with tans and new clothes and accents they claim to have "just developed" in the weeks they were away.

We never leave. We've been in our suite in the upper dorms since we got here, a single-story concrete building with ancient couches in the lobby. We tell everyone we don't go home for the summer because Ellison is boring, but the truth is, we don't go home because there isn't a home to go to—there's just an empty house in Georgia and an uncle in

California who sends us an allowance from our father's estate every month. We were the last of ten children—our parents were already old when we were born, and most of our brothers were long out of the house. Our mother didn't live to see us start second grade, and raising daughters alone scared our father—not that it mattered much, since his Alzheimer's meant he'd forgotten us before we made it through our first year here. I read his past once. Thousands of memories, bright, vivid, colorful. I described them to our father while Anne and Jane watched eagerly, convinced that this would fix everything, that he'd remember us, that we'd be a family.

It didn't work. He didn't recognize his own memories. He didn't know them.

He didn't know us. It was the only time my power seemed useful, and it failed me.

Technically, I guess there is something more than our empty house, faraway uncle, the brothers we barely know: There's our father, sitting in a nursing home in Atlanta, with no idea who his children are. So as far as Anne, Jane, and I are concerned, we are alone in the world, except for one another.

I sneak into the dorm's main door, shivering at the blast of air-conditioning. The hallways smell like pine cleaning solution until I get to the end, where our apartment door is, and the smells of clothes and perfume and life mingle with the chemical. I unlock the door and push it open—Anne's and Jane's purses are on the kitchen counter. They must have thought I went to bed early—they'd never have gone to sleep if they realized I wasn't home. I slip into my bedroom—it's tiny, but then, all the bedrooms here are. *Maybe I should wake up my sisters and tell them what happened*, I think as I pull off my clothes. With Jude, with Naida—but how could I possibly explain Naida to them? A naked girl who came out of the water and went back into it, her memories of screaming. I'm afraid to try to explain her, afraid of the fact that I *can't* explain her.

I fall back onto my unmade bed, tangle my legs into the sheets, and close my eyes. Maybe she was a dream. Maybe when I wake up, I'll realize there was just the boy. Nothing more. No one else.

• ◆ •

My dreams are full of screams and waves, boys falling into the arms of girls in the ocean. When I open my eyes and realize my room is flooded with sunlight, I feel like I've been tricked—how have I possibly been home for hours? It feels like one, at the most. Regardless of how long I was out, sleeping didn't do what I'd hoped—I still remember Naida perfectly, well enough to know for certain that she was real, even though I don't know who or what she is. Just thinking about her makes my head hurt.

I can never fall back asleep once I've woken up, so I begrudgingly get out of bed. My hair is still stringy and ragged from the ocean water last night, and I have scrapes from the sand on my legs that I didn't notice before. I sigh, tie my hair into a ponytail, and open my bedroom door—

"Whoa. What happened to you?" Anne says before I have time to process where she's sitting. I blink blearily—she's at the bar, eating a gigantic bowl of cereal, hair wet but combed out from a recent shower.

"Nothing. I mean…" I sigh, shaking my head. "A guy fell off the pier. I ran down to the beach to help." We don't lie to one another as a general rule—after Jane's power developed, there was no point, since she could read our minds. Still, omitting the truth about Naida seems so, so much simpler right now.

"Wow," Anne says. She looks over at Jane, who's sitting on the couch with her legs drawn up.

"Did he survive?" Jane asks.

"He's fine. I went with him to the hospital."

"You can do that?" Jane says. "I thought only family could ride with the paramedic. Was he hot?"

"The paramedic?"

"No, the guy you saved," Anne says, even though Jane asked the original question.

The guy I saved. There's that word again, *saved*. I try to ignore it, thinking instead about Jude's face. He had long eyelashes, I remember that, and hair that was streaked from the sunlight to become the exact color that some girls pay money for. Handsome, though? He was nearly dead.

"No one's hot when they're drowning," I argue, walking into the kitchen to scrounge up my own breakfast. Anne took the last of the cereal, so I start making a peanut butter sandwich.

"And anyone stupid enough to fall off the pier isn't hot at all," Anne says. "I prefer smart guys."

"That's so not true," Jane argues.

"It is! The guys we pick up don't count. I'm talking, if I were going to fall in love, it'd be with a smart guy," Anne says, rolling her eyes at Jane. "Think you'll be in the newspaper?" she continues.

"I doubt it."

"What if he's, like, a millionaire's son, though? And you saved him," Jane says, twirling her hair. "Maybe then we can afford a real apartment instead of this place." She gestures at our suite. It's really not that bad—it is an apartment, practically. It's just that it's still in a dorm, a fact that Anne and Jane find incredibly irritating. Actually, they find school in general irritating—why learn math when you have secret powers?

"He wasn't a millionaire's son. Don't get excited. He's a musician from Lake City, he's broke—"

"You *read* him? While he was drowning? Get anything interesting?" Anne asks.

"No. I didn't even mean to read him, it just . . . happened," I say, taking the first bite of my sandwich and shrugging.

"See, if you used your power more, you'd learn to control it," Jane says in a voice that makes me want to yell at her. She's right, though—they can control their powers better than I can, in large part because of their nights of "practicing."

But regardless of Jane's voice, I don't yell at her *or* Anne—and they don't yell at me. In fact, we don't fight, really. We just disagree. Not like Jude—he fights with his family, all the time. Or, fought with them. He doesn't talk to them anymore. I didn't see exactly why—I pulled away from him too quickly. I wonder about his family, about who would have told them if he'd died last night.

Who would have told my sisters if it'd been me?

Jane grabs my arm. "Oh, god, Celia, you're so morbid," she moans, releasing me.

"Hey," I snap, leaning away. Panic rises in my throat—did she see Naida?

"Relax, you weren't answering Anne's question, and I just wanted to know why," she says, shrugging, like she merely pulled my hair.

"What question?" I ask, glaring at Anne, who I'm pleased to see looks frustrated with Jane. She shakes her head before speaking.

"I was asking if you're going to see him again. The guy you saved," she repeats.

"No. Why would I?"

"Because you saved his life! He owes you a—what's it called? A blood debt." Anne's eyes are glimmering, like we're writing a story instead of discussing someone's drowning.

"He's not bad-looking, either," Jane adds. I turn to her, and she giggles. "You were still thinking about his face! I didn't mean to. He's not, like, movie-star hot, but he has that sort of indie look going for him."

"Go see him," Anne insists. "What else do you have to do?"

"You know I don't like to talk to people I've read!"

"Which probably explains why you only talk to us," Anne answers.

The thing about Anne is, she doesn't necessarily win an argument. She just wears you down, beats at your edges until it's easier to give in than it is to fight her. And she's not wrong—I don't really talk to anyone other than my sisters. She just doesn't understand that it's with good reason. Why would I talk to people, get to know them, when the slightest touch means knowing their strongest memories? Sometimes it's not terrible, I guess, when the strongest memory is something beautiful, but so often it's not....I've told Anne this before. She doesn't understand, though, and so she'll wear me down instead of trying. What can I say? She was the firstborn of the three of us. Maybe that's why she's the strongest.

"Maybe I'll go today. I don't know," I answer. "I'll need the car." I'm hoping the last point will persuade them to drop it—when we were only eleven, Anne predicted that I would wreck our car. Ever since, she and Jane have been wary of letting me drive it, even though I'm the only one without a speeding ticket to my name. Anne's power is almost a sure thing, though; even when she tries to intervene, the futures she reads almost always come to pass. She says that's because the future is like tangled string—you might be able to see how it ends, but it's almost impossible to work out the knots and figure out how it got there. And apparently there are an awful lot of knots between me and a wrecked car.

They look at each other, weighing the worthiness of me

behind the wheel with their desire for scandal. "Ugh, fine," Jane says. "But can we come?" *Damn. Not the response I was hoping for.*

"Probably not. I don't even know if they'll let me in to see him. Last night it was just a special circumstance, since I...I saved him."

"Well, if he turns out to be awesome, you have to take us eventually," Jane says, as if I just ruined her plans for the day. I avoid them for the next few hours, Jane especially, because I have no intention to actually go see Jude. But there is something I plan to do—go back to the beach. Look for Naida.

I don't really want to. The more I think about her, the more afraid I am of her. And I wasn't lying to Anne—I don't enjoy seeing people I've read. But as much as I liked Jude's memories, I know I can force myself to forget him. As much as Naida's mind scared me, confused me, I know I won't be able to forget her. I won't be able to forget the way she disappeared into the water, and I won't be able to forget the way she looked at me when I called her name—like she didn't know it. Like she was a wild thing, and I was calling her as if she were tame. There must be an explanation, and maybe if I see her again, I'll understand, and I can forget.

I leave for the beach in the early evening, an hour or so before the sun will start setting. Jane, thinking I'm meeting Jude, hassles me for not wearing a dress, but I manage to stave her off with excuses about hurrying to arrive before visiting hours at the hospital are over. I jump in the car and leave before she can "accidentally" touch me and realize I'm lying.

57

Our car is a hand-me-down, bought for dirt cheap off a boy Anne charmed. It rattles, and the sunshine-yellow paint job is splotchy, but it runs. Anne and Jane don't like to be seen in it, and to be entirely honest, it's not something I'd proudly identify as my own. But it does the job, so that's enough, I suppose. I take the long way through town to avoid the inevitable traffic at the amusement center that's always packed with waterslide-hungry kids, and to stall a little bit longer....

Eventually I have to park. I do so at the Pavilion—it's closed during the day, but I see a handful of employees setting up for the evening. Down the pier, I can see police tape sectioning off the back end, where the lifted board that caused Jude to trip is astonishingly visible in the daylight. I walk past the pier's mouth and take the same road down to the beach that I took last night. It's hardly a road at all, just rocks and sand and sea grass, and the ground shifts under your feet with every step. Farther down the beach, where the water and the sky blur together to form a misty violet-colored line, I can see shapes of people, hundreds of them playing in the water. Bright orange circles—umbrellas—dot the shore, and every now and then the wind stops and the tiniest sampling of laughter and conversation reaches me.

I drop a towel in the sand and sit by the old church, leaning my back against its graffiti-laden wall. I try to figure out exactly where I was standing last night, exactly where the ambulance drove off, where Naida ran into the water leaving only a trail of bloody footprints. It's impossible, though—the tide has eaten all evidence that anyone was ever here.

The sun begins to set; every second the water reflects a new color. Peaches and yellows and purples and bright, almost neon pink. They make the ocean look like it's being iced with the colors of the sky above, yet underneath those highlights, the water is blacker than ever. I stare into the water like it might toss Naida out at me, like it cares that I'm here against my better judgment, like it will reward me for coming back.

It doesn't.

CHAPTER SIX

Lo

I wake up with a jolt. Have I lost it?
No. *Naida.* I exhale, turn over on my stomach. The sand
grinds beneath me, cradling my body. It's nearly dusk, based
on the amount of light peering through the water. The other
girls are talking, a few of the youngest halfheartedly playing
with a crab that's poking out from under the *Glasgow*'s hull.
It bares its claws; they taunt it into snapping at them and
laugh so quietly it's almost not laughter at all but just another
sound in the ocean. Pity we haven't seen whales in ages.
They're so big, they make me feel small, remind me of how
large the ocean is, that it holds creatures like them. And
they'll play games, sort of, if you can get them to stay under
long enough. I wish we could talk to them, ask them how
they manage to go from the depths to the surface so often. . . .
My eyes fall on Molly. She's sitting on a jagged plank that
juts out from the ship's broken center and is staring at her

feet. She looks different than yesterday. Her skin isn't quite as pink, her hair not quite as red. She looks sad, beautifully sad, and I can't help but realize that both of us, in one way or another, are alone right now. I rise and move toward her.

Molly looks up, and any sadness is replaced by bitterness. She's glaring, eyes bright and sharp. I look down, turn away from her. I understand why she's angry, especially now that I remember my old name, but I can't help her. I ignore the feeling of her eyes searing into my back and rise to join the old ones. They're sitting on the *Glasgow*'s deck, staring into the distance, as per usual.

"Lo," one says quietly to me as I approach. She hasn't been old for very long, but she's already so beautiful. Her skin is the color of the ocean at winter and looks smooth, like glass that's been worn down by the water. I used to know her name. Ry, I think, but I can't really remember.

"Hello," I answer. Before I can stop myself, I wonder what her human name was. If I could find out for her, would she want to know? No. Of course not. She's happy here, growing old, growing beautiful. Each of us ages differently—plenty of girls who arrived after me have already grown old and joined those in the air. How much time does this girl have left among us?

"What do you see?" I ask the old one, looking in the direction of her gaze. She's sitting on a raised portion of the deck, an area I've always found eerie because of the faces that stare at me from the remaining railings—every arm's length, a cherub's face is carved into the wood. Most are only half faces or blank faces now, but a few full sets of eyes watch as I sit down beside her.

She doesn't answer at first, then turns to me. "Nothing," she says. "It's beautiful."

The old ones often don't make sense to the rest of us, but we know they do, in fact, make sense, if only to themselves. Key says they learn secrets from the water, secrets we can only learn with age—something we're all envious of from time to time. I leave the old one, but I'm not sure she notices that I've left. I linger near the edge of the crowd of other girls, growing closer to the *Glasgow*. Surely they won't notice I'm gone, if I go to the surface for a moment. It'll be all right. I'll take one breath of dry air—maybe that will help me remember more about Naida. Then I'll come back, and Key and I will braid each other's hair, and then we'll race around and stop, fast, so that we keep drifting even though we aren't moving. It'll be just like normal.

This will only take a moment. One moment.

I jet off for the surface, swimming away from the rest of us and up at once. What will they do if they see me? They don't follow the old ones. I can't imagine them following me.

I hesitate at the surface. If I break it, if I breathe in, I can't pretend it never happened.

If I don't break it, I'll always wonder about the name, the past, the girl on the shore.

I slowly lift my eyes out of the water. I squint, blink as my eyelashes clump together. I feel wrong, I feel terrible, I feel traitorous, even, as I look at the horizon and see the slight blue shape of the shore. *I've come this far. . . .*

I swim forward just under the surface, emerging every so often to see the giant wooden pillars that support the pier becoming clearer. Before long, I've crossed over the sandbar and am exactly where I was last night—the ocean has changed, of course, and there are no markers, but I still know where I am. I suppose when you know a place as well as we know the ocean, you're never lost, no matter how the water changes.

I lift my head out of the water again; hair clings to my face, drips a curtain of water in front of my eyes. I rise a little higher—can anyone see me? No, there's no one here. The shore is empty, as is the pier. Farther inland, I can see the sun setting. It's beautiful, a bright red-orange that's just starting to vanish into the tree line, like it's falling into the land. It burns—we never surface during the day, and it's so much brighter than I remember. Still, I can't look away. I stare at the sun until my eyes fill with water and my cheeks feel burned, like they're drying up.

Remember, remember. I repeat Naida's name to myself— no, *my name* to myself. It's my name, and they're my memories hidden deep below the surface. The same way my sisters are hidden beneath the waves right now. Hidden doesn't mean gone.

Nothing comes. I duck down into the water and swim closer to the pier, going from pillar to pillar until I'm almost by the shore. I close my eyes and plant one foot onto the sand.

It doesn't hurt, but then, I'm still in water up to my head. I take a step forward, another, another.

The feeling of a knife slicing into the soft part of my foot starts when the water is waist-deep. I look down, see the tendrils of blood spiraling up. Another step, another. The salt water burns the wound. I don't want to put my foot down, but...another. There's a halo of red water around me now, and for a moment the ground seems to get softer. But no, it isn't the ground, it's the torn-up skin on my feet. I think it's shredding away.

I cry out when I take another step and can't force myself to take any more. I tumble forward, pull myself the last little distance onto the shore with my hands. There's a trail of blood behind me, a perfect line that the waves quickly destroy. I watch as my blood washes away, becomes just another part of the ocean.

And I still don't remember anything. I exhale, cough—my lungs feel strangely light, empty of the water, the warm weight I've grown used to. Inhale a few deep breaths; it's not comfortable—I can tell I won't be able to breathe air like this for long, but I can bear it for the time being. I sigh, fall back in the shadow of the pier—I remember watching the boy with the gray eyes fall from here just last night, when everything was perfect and I was just a girl waiting to become an angel. This is stupid—why am I here? I'm not made to be on the shore. I can't get my soul back, I can't make a boy love me, and I can't remember my past. How could someone without a soul remember what it felt like to have one? That's like asking each drop in the ocean to remember its time as rain. It was a lifetime ago. It was a soul ago, a soul I'm perfectly happy without, if it's indeed already gone. I inhale deep again, grimace at the dryness of my lungs, the pain in my feet. I'm not meant for this world.

I hear something above the sound of the waves, a scratching noise. I lean my head back and look toward a building on the shore, the one that looked like a ghost last night—

A girl.

There's a girl—she's looking at me. She sees me. She sees me, I have to go, I have to go back. Instinct overpowers everything else in me, and I rise and force myself to my feet, groan in pain as I run into the water. I collapse when it's just deep enough for me to swim, grateful at the way it cradles me, at how comfortable it is compared with the land. I'm about to dive. The girl is running toward the water's edge—

She calls my name. *My* name. Naida.

CHAPTER SEVEN

❧

Celia

She's here.

I see her in the water, by the pier. If I wasn't looking for her, I'm sure I would have missed her—her skin is grayish, her hair dark brown and heavy-looking. She moves with the waves, the way that seagulls do when they sit on the water. She dives, reemerges, drawing closer, closer to the shore. And then she starts to walk.

Every step she takes looks deliberate, like she's walking on a high wire instead of up to dry sand. As she gets closer I think I know why—the expression on her face is pure pain. Her mouth widens into a grimace. I rise, keeping my back against the church.

I'm not sure what to do. I'm not even sure what she is. A mermaid? No. Mermaids have tails. *And don't exist.*

Just like triplets with powers don't exist.

She finally makes it onto the shore, collapses. Even from

here, I can see the blood running from her feet, making tiny rivers that are destroyed with each new wave. She looks limp and broken, like the ocean stole her bones and threw her out. Each time a wave sweeps far enough onto the sand to touch her toes, I see her quiver, try to cling to the water that so quickly slides back where it came from.

She is frightening, but she is also helpless. And staring at her lying there certainly won't help me get her out of my head. I swallow and start toward her, kicking up dry sand and squinting against the reflection of the almost-set sun on the waves. She turns her head up toward me, and I see her eyes—dark, gray like stones—widen. She forces herself up shakily, moves toward the water. Her legs buckle under her with every step, like they're broken, and there's the blood again, though it's now dark and thick. She makes it to where the water is shoulder-deep and falls in, and suddenly, it's like she's home. Her body slips under, every bit as graceful as a dolphin. She's leaving, I have to—

"Naida!" I call her name. Again and again, I yell as I watch her dark form start away from the shore.

And then stop.

I've reached the edge of the water. I drop my hands to my knees and pant while trying to keep my eyes on her. She's still, she's listening. "Naida," I say. "I'm not...I..." What am I, exactly? I'm not going to hurt her? I'm more worried about her hurting me, to be honest. Say something, though, anything....

"I met you last night," I call. "I just want to talk."

About the scream in your head. About why your memories are different from everyone else's. I want to talk to you so I can forget about you.

I see her turn against the waves. She slowly lifts her head out of the water.

She is beautiful—more so now that she's in the water. Her skin is not quite as gray up close, but around her ears, her hairline, her shoulder bones is a light bluish color, like she's very cold. Everything about her matches the sea, except her hair—it has the slightest hint of chocolate brown in it, like it would be better suited to a forest.

"Please. Talk to me," I say, finally standing up straight again. The lights on the pier flicker on automatically with the encroaching darkness. Her head snaps toward them, and for a minute, I think she's going to vanish again.

"It hurts."

I almost can't hear her at first, over the sound of the waves, but I manage to understand what she said. I don't respond, because I have no idea how to.

"It hurts to walk on land. It cuts me. It's like knives," she says. There's no inflection in her voice, no happiness or sorrow, only a single note that bounces through every word.

"Can you come any closer? So I can hear you better, at least?" I call out. She considers this, then obliges, creeping closer before sitting down where the waves are knee-deep. I nod, then sit in the wet sand where the tiniest remains of waves lap up, soaking my shorts and covering my toes with sand.

She stares at me. She doesn't blink, and I know if I were

to stand suddenly, run toward her, yell, that she'd be into the deep water so quickly that I wouldn't even make it a step before she was gone.

She's waiting for me to speak, I can tell. I'm unpracticed at starting conversations—that's Anne's job, and less often, Jane's. But...

"You left last night," I say. The words sound stunted.

"I didn't want to be seen."

"I'd already seen you."

"That was necessary. The boy would have drowned," she says, as if this is obvious.

"That's right. You saved him," I say. "You pulled him out of the water."

"You breathed for him," she says, shaking her head. "I'm glad he's alive. He didn't need to die." She pauses for a long time, but doesn't look away from me, like she's waiting for something.

"You... you live in the water?" I finally manage. The words sound stupid when they fall from my mouth, clunky.

"Yes. Now," she says dismissively, and then her tone grows more serious. "But not before. Before I was this, I was Naida. You *knew* the name Naida."

She might be able to maintain eye contact with me, but I'm not as strong—I look down. The fact that she came from the water, that she's *something* different, someone different, that doesn't seem to matter. Am I going to admit my power to a stranger? It seems wrong, wrong in every way, and yet... "Yes," I answer.

"Did you know her?" she asks, and for the first time there's the tiniest bit of inflection, of curiosity in her voice.

I raise an eyebrow, a little confused. "No. I've never met you before. But..." I inhale. "Sometimes when I touch people, I know things they've lived through." My voice falters, like it can't bear the fact that I'm admitting my power—despite downplaying it quite a bit—aloud.

Her eyes widen. "You know about her life?"

"*Your* life," I say, though it's more of a question than a statement. "What...what are you? How do you live in the water?"

She continues to stare at me, like this is something she's never considered before. "The same way everything else lives in the water. We're not like you. But I was, back when I was Naida."

"Wait, you *were* Naida? Who are you now?"

"Lo. My name is Lo, for a while."

"I don't understand." The sky has turned purple, like there's a haze over the beach. The scent of cotton candy drifts down from the Pavilion, but with the tail end of the pier closed off, there still aren't any other people to see us. Naida—Lo, whoever she is, does the closest thing to a shrug I think she can manage.

"I don't, either. Something changed. I used to be a human named Naida. And now I'm not, and my name is Lo. We all used to be human, but now we're not."

"We?"

Her eyes darken a bit, an expression I recognize—it's the

70

way Anne looks if someone slights me or Jane. It's protective, it's cautious. She finally answers. "My sisters. They're like me."

"How did you become...this, if you used to be human?"

"We don't know for certain. An angel brought us here."

"An angel?"

"Yes," she says dismissively, shakes when a gust of wind sweeps across us. "You know my human name because you touched me?"

I tense a little, but nod.

"Do you know anything else?"

"Not very much," I answer—it seems too early to mention the scream. "Your memories are strange; it's like they're hidden. What do you remember from being...Naida?"

Her gaze becomes unfocused for a moment, but she shakes her head. She looks sad, mournful, like someone has died. "There was more last night, but I've forgotten it again. I can't hold on to it."

"I can..." Am I really going to do this? I swallow. "I can help you. I have to touch you again, though," I add quickly. What am I doing? First I tell her about my power; now I'm using it on her? I don't want to see the pain in her head, I don't want to hear the scream again, but...

My power has only failed me before this. But now it's worth something. Now it's needed....How could I walk away, especially from the girl who saved Jude's life—the girl whose credit I stole?

Lo looks at me, though I don't think she's debating

whether or not to do it—I think she's having trouble believing it's possible. It seems odd, that a girl who claims to live underwater would find something like reading memories strange. She extends an arm; she wants me to come to her.

"I promise not to drown you," she says sincerely. The possibility hadn't occurred to me, but it manages to entirely replace the fear of using my power. I cringe and creep closer. She watches me, intrigued, and I remember how effortlessly she moved through the waves. Closer, I can see that her arms are faintly patterned in a way that makes me think of lichen on trees. She inhales as I reach out, and I see her teeth are slightly pointed.

I'm afraid to close my eyes, though I want to so, so badly.

I clamp my fingers down on her slick forearm.

The scream echoes through my mind, so strong that for a moment I think Lo is actually screaming aloud. Blackness, blackness is everywhere, a fog of dark and unknown with only the name *Naida* and the fading sound of a girl screaming. Lo whispers something, but I ignore her. *Focus, Celia.* I give in and close my eyes, try to look the way Anne and Jane do when they touch boys on the pier.

The darkness in her head starts to clear ever so slightly, flashes of memories that are buried deep. A house, a man, a woman, a town—

"What do you see?" Lo's voice finally breaks through the barrage of images in my head.

"There's a girl. She has dark brown hair. She's pretty. And a kitchen, with green doors that lead into it and—"

I was going to keep going, but Lo snatches her arm away. My eyes shoot open. I'm ready to run, ready to scream for help, though I'm not sure if I'd be yelling for myself or for her. She's staring at me like I've said something wrong, but then her eyes widen. She exhales, her breath shakes, her eyes dart around in a way entirely different from her eerie stillness. She shudders and falls forward into the water, with none of the grace she had before. Before I can stop myself, I reach out, grab her under her arms, and pull her face back out of the ocean. She coughs, chokes, and looks up at me. Her eyes are less gray than before, more hazel.

"I remember," she says.

CHAPTER EIGHT

⑥

Naida

Am I dreaming?

The world seems wrong and mixed up and different from the one that I know to be real, so it could be a dream. I inhale; the bite of salty air fills my lungs.

That felt real. I look down—my hands are strange, the wrong color, like I've been picking blueberries and haven't washed them. I stare at them for a moment, turn them over, and inspect my palms. Everything feels real, but something isn't right....

And then I realize I'm naked. Naked, kneeling in the ocean. I look up at the girl in front of me, try to cover my chest with my arms.

"Lo?" she asks. She looks scared.

Lo. Something inside me sparks, recognizes the name.... I am Lo. But that's not my real name; that's not who I really am. I shake my head. "Naida?" she whispers, and I nod.

"I..." I look down at the waves washing around me, embarrassed—at least we're here alone.

"I've got a towel up there," she says, pointing toward an old building—a church, I think, or some sort of temple. "Do you want it?" I nod. I know how I got here, I know I've been underwater, and yet I feel like the name Lo and the ocean full of girls are just a strange nighttime fantasy, that just yesterday I was...

Where was I? I can remember the house. It was also a store. We sold things; we sold food—I remember the smell of vanilla and cinnamon. The girl takes my forearm with her hand and starts to lead me forward—I eagerly take a step.

I cry out loud, almost fall to my knees. Pain shoots up through my feet, like it's prying the bones of my feet apart, like it's burning them. With it come memories, memories of the world underwater, of a sunken ship, of being someone else—of being Lo.

"Wait here," the girl says. She frowns at me, then jogs away to get the towel while I'm left standing in the surf.

Not Lo, not Lo. She feels like another person lurking in my head. I don't want to be her. I try my best to cast her memories away. Think about something else—the house, the house I lived in, and the forest around it, the way it went on forever. So far from the ocean that the world smelled of pine trees and heat. Just as I remember it, though, the memory starts to fade, and I realize I can't quite remember what pine sap smells like. Salt? No, I'm getting confused; that's just what I smell right now. Pines are different; they have spindly needles and layered bark. I think. Why can't I remember?

The girl returns with the towel, wraps it around me. I look at the shore longingly—I want to sit in the sand, I want my body to dry out entirely, but Lo's voice is in the back of my head: *No, no, I live in the water. I can't go on land like that—*

"Naida," the girl says, and I force Lo away. "Do you remember now?" She touches my shoulder, and her eyes change, get distant, like she sees something I don't see.

How could I forget the scent of pine trees? They were all over the place in the woods surrounding our house. They shed so many needles that sometimes the ground looked like a red-brown carpet, and during summer thunderstorms, they swayed and thrashed against one another like giants at war.

I want to sit down. I wince and force myself to walk forward. My vision goes bright from the pain. The girl pauses, then loops my right arm over her shoulders. Walking still hurts, but with most of my weight on her, it's not quite as bad. As soon as we make it to dry sand, I collapse, staring at the trail of my blood leading back to the water.

"Who are you?" I ask her.

"My name's Celia," the girl answers. "Celia Reynolds. We met last night—"

"I remember that," I reply. "Sort of. It feels like it didn't really happen, though."

"I know exactly what you mean," Celia answers, words slightly muttered.

"All my memories feel real—but they aren't complete. There are parts missing."

"Like what?"

"Like the faces," I answer slowly. It's getting dark now; the sun is out of sight over the palmettos behind us, but remnants of its light still cling to the sky. My hands don't look quite as wrong now, though I'm not sure if it's because I'm drier or because it's darker. I look out over the water, try to remember the faces of my family, of the people I lived with. I can see their hair, dark chocolate brown, but that's it. Their faces are blurry, their voices distorted save for the occasional laugh or when they say my name. I realize I remember exactly how my name sounded on their tongues.

"Do you remember your last name?" Celia asks. I shake my head. "Do you remember...something frightening?"

"What do you mean?"

"When I..." She pauses, swallows. "When I look at your memories, the loudest one is a memory of someone...of someone screaming. It's so loud it almost covers the rest of them up. I can't see it clearly."

Maybe that should scare me, but it doesn't—how can I be scared of something that I don't remember? I wish I did. I wish I had all the pieces. She can find a scream in my mind that I can't. It doesn't seem fair.

"Who am I?" I ask, not exactly to Celia, though I hope she has an answer.

Celia shakes her head. "I don't know. Thirty minutes ago, you told me you were Lo."

"I am," I answer. "But that feels like a nickname. Like a fake name I give people, because my real name is Naida. It's always been Naida. Naida..." My last name, it was on the tip of my tongue, it was there... but it's gone. "I don't remember anything. Bits and pieces of things, but nothing big. Nothing real." I look at Celia desperately, and she reaches out to touch me again, closes her eyes. It takes her a few minutes. She moves her hand up and down my arm like she's reading something beneath my skin.

"I think..." she starts quietly, like she's not certain. "You have sisters. Or, one sister? It feels like there are two, but I never see the other's face, never see any sign of her. I must be reading things wrong—"

"I have one sister," I say, inhaling sharply. My older sister. She taught me how to French braid and painted my face like a cat every Halloween, since that's all I ever wanted to go as.

"And there's a sign, on the door of your house. I think it's your name, I think it's—"

"Kelly." The word falls off my tongue simply, perfectly. "That's my last name. Naida Kelly."

"Right," Celia says. She releases my arm, shudders like touching me hurt her. "Sorry," she says when she notices me looking. "I've never done it on purpose before. It isn't really fun, looking into people's pasts, and that... that scream..."

I nod, then stare out over the ocean. That's where Lo lives—that's her home. Sounds drift down from somewhere above the pier, melodies and hums and generators buzzing. A carnival, it sounds like. I want to go, but . . . I can't walk. I'm naked. I'm Naida, but I still look like Lo.

"Can you help me remember anything else?" I ask Celia.

"Maybe. It's hard to tell," Celia says. "It's strange—everything in your head is dark. I think the more you remember, the more I see to help you remember, especially since that scream is in my way."

"But there's more, right? There are more memories there, somewhere?"

"Yes," Celia says. "People block out memories all the time, but they're always there. Even people with Alzheimer's, the memories are still there. . . ." She drifts off, like she's said more than she wanted.

The tide has been creeping in as we talk; it won't reach us, exactly, but it's close enough now that occasionally we feel the ocean's spray. The sky is dark blue, balancing on the edge of night. I keep trying to dig deeper in my memories, see more, but all I can get are glimpses, tiny flashes. Then Celia touches me again, tells me about something she sees in my mind, and it jump-starts my own recollections. Still, they only go so far. After another hour, it's clear that I've remembered all I can—and besides, Celia is starting to look worn from digging through my mind. I feel guilty, move a little away from her so she doesn't have to touch me again, even accidentally.

But despite all that, in the back of my head, there's always the ocean—not the one here, the surface of the ocean that everyone sees. There's the hidden world, the place deep underwater where everything is cold. There's Lo. She gets louder and louder, aching to slip into the waves. She is me, and yet she isn't—it's like we're forced to share this body. *My* body. I squeeze my eyes shut to try to ignore her, but a moment later, my gaze is cast over the sea. Lo is stronger than me right now, her urge to return to the waves more powerful than my longing to stay here. We aren't even fighting, yet I know she'll win.

My eyes burn from salt and tears. "I can't stay here."

"What do you mean?"

"The water. I've got to get back in the water—no. *She* has to get back in the water. She needs it to live...."

"Are you sure?" Celia asks. "I could talk to my sisters, maybe.... Our dorm is sort of close.... Can you leave the shore?"

"I don't know," I say, frustrated. "I don't know anything. It's just...she's pulling me to her home, and I don't think I can ignore her much longer."

Celia looks down, shakes her head, like she can't believe what she's about to say. "I can come back. If you want. In a few days, maybe?"

"Yes," I say instantly. "I'd like that. Please."

Celia nods, looks like she's readying herself for battle. I exhale, rise, wince as the pain shoots through my feet. She moves to help me, but I dodge her hands—she shouldn't have to touch me, have to remember for me again. I grimace and awkwardly slide the towel off my body. Celia takes it and looks away.

Lo knows how the ocean works. She knows how to dive into the water. But as I walk forward, I'm afraid. This isn't my world. It isn't right, it isn't—

I sigh involuntarily when the first wave brushes around my feet, soothing the pain. Another step, another, and with each one I feel better—like I was sick and I'm being healed. When I get thigh-deep, an especially large wave crashes in front of me. It almost knocks me backward, sweeps me back to the shore, but then it's perfect, it's beautiful, it holds me like it loves me. I fall forward, and the water envelops me, swirls my hair around me like a blanket. There's no pain. There's nothing but simplicity, nothing but beauty as I slip away from the shore and dive deep, deep into the ocean, into the silence, into the cool water and the smooth sand that coats the ocean floor.

CHAPTER NINE

Celia

I feel shaken, confused when I get back to the dorm. There's still sand stuck to my legs and salt coating my hair, and my cheeks are raw from the wind.

I don't like reading memories. I don't like carrying anyone else's burdens, don't like seeing the things so horrible that even they've blocked them out. And I certainly don't like intentionally doing it. But the look on Naida's—Lo's?—face when I helped her remember.... It was like each memory was a breath, something that sustained her till the next one. I never thought my power could be useful. What if I can help Lo remember Naida? What if I can bring Naida back entirely?

Lo scares me. She lives in the water, for starters—something I still have trouble believing—and the way she talks.... It's disconcerting, like she's a very old person in a young body. And yet, Naida is someone I could be friends with. Naida is someone who needs me. My power can help her in a way even Anne's and Jane's couldn't; my silly, useless power might turn out to do a greater good than theirs combined....

And she's forgetting her past. I think of my father, of the blank look in his eyes when I tried to help him remember. No one should forget their past; no one should lose their memories. Not if I can stop it.

I drop my bag on the counter with a sigh and realize Anne and Jane are still out. They're likely at the Pavilion, by the place I just left—yes, when I check my phone, I see a text from Anne suggesting I join them there. Then another, advising me to bring the boy I saved. I roll my eyes, wonder how I'll explain why I didn't see him tonight. I can't tell them about Naida, can I? My secret with her seems as sacred as the one between Anne, Jane, and me. But they're my sisters. I can't keep it from them forever.

I get in the shower, fight with the dozens of shampoos and cleansers and conditioners that line the side of the tub, then head to the couch with my hair still wet. I slept in too late to be tired at midnight, but I want to do something mindless, something to help me forget that I saw a girl run into the ocean and vanish less than an hour ago. I turn on the television, find a movie, and stare at the screen until the people start to look like shapes and the words sound like noises. When the phone rings, I don't hear it at first—it takes several rounds before I blearily sit up. A number I don't recognize—I sigh and answer the call.

83

"Hello?"

"Hi, this is...this is weird, but is your name Celia?"

"Yes, who is this?" It's after I've said it that I recognize his voice—I didn't hear it out loud at much more than a whisper, but I heard it in his memories.

"Hi. My name is Jude Wallace, and I believe you saved my life last night."

"I...yes..."

"Well, I was calling to say thanks, which sounded a lot more genuine and less lame before I said it out loud, and now I think I just sound like a lunatic. I'm not crazy—I sneaked a look at my chart at the hospital, and your information was on it and...yeah."

I laugh a little. This is easier than talking to someone in person, where I worry they might brush past me, might come too close, might share their memories without meaning to. "It was nothing," I say. "The paramedics did all the work."

"They say you pulled me out and did CPR. That's not nothing. Trust me, my lungs would know if you'd done nothing."

"Well...you're welcome, then?" What do you say to something like this?

"What's especially stupid about all this is I've noticed that plank and avoided it hundreds of times before—I play at the pier every night during the summer. I don't know what happened," he says. "*And* I lost my guitar in the water. Which I know in the grand scheme of things isn't a big deal, but now I have to play with my crappy one until I can get a new one."

"How long will that take?"

"Based on my calculations, I'll have a new one by the time I'm forty-seven," he jokes, and I laugh again. "Just kidding. Not too long, though it'll pretty much destroy my savings account. And my non-savings account. And the quarters I find in my car seats." He talks fast, as if he doesn't like the chance of silence creeping into the conversation.

"Well, um...let me know if there's anything I can do to help," I say. "Beyond, you know—the CPR."

"What if you were to go get lunch with me?"

The door bangs. Anne and Jane stumble in, tripping over their own feet, lips red and dresses short. They're laughing loudly till they see me waving my arms, trying to make them shut up.

"How would that help?" I ask, distracted as Anne and Jane mouth "Who is it?" almost simultaneously.

"Well, for starters, it would absolve me of the incredible guilt I'm feeling for thanking someone who saved my life over the phone. If I'm not focusing on guilt, I'll work harder. I'll make more money. I'll get a guitar sooner. Doves will fly free, and soldiers will lay down their guns."

"I don't know...." I say. Not that I don't want to see him, actually—I just feel like I'm dealing with enough at the moment, without adding him to the picture.

"It's the guy! The one she saved!" Jane deduces excitedly.

"Who was that?" Jude asks.

"My sister," I explain.

"Well, bring her, too, then," he says, and I cringe. "That way if I turn out to be weird, you have backup."

"No, that's not it—"

"Then come on. Lunch. Please? I'll buy. Well, obviously I'll buy, since it's a 'thanks for saving me' lunch, but . . . yeah."

"There're two of them."

"Lunches?"

"Sisters."

"Bring them both," Jude suggests. I wish he knew exactly what he was saying. Anne is thrown over the couch, ear pressed as close to the phone as she can get without touching her bare arm to mine. She giggles loudly.

"Okay, right, where and when?" I say, grimacing. I just want to get off the phone.

"Maybe Wednesday? Have you ever been to that Thai place in the Landing?"

"We love it!" Anne says, and Jane laughs as she grabs Diet Cokes from the refrigerator for both of them.

"Okay. Then . . . Wednesday. One o'clock?"

"We'll be there. Thanks. Bye," I say unceremoniously, and hang up while glaring at my sisters.

"Oh, come on, Celia, we were just playing," Jane says, opening the soda can. She's drunk, or close to it.

"Besides, that conversation sounds like you didn't see him today. Where were you?" Anne asks. She's grinning, but there's a sharpness to her words.

I shake my head at her. "I was out. Without you."

"Clearly, but where—"

"I didn't ask the two of you where you were when you came in," I point out, rising and pocketing my phone.

"Yeah, but that's because we were *together*," Anne says.

We're stronger together.

I was strong on my own. For the first time.

"I was out," I say, and turn away from them. I walk to my tiny bedroom, shut the door briskly—I can practically feel the two of them exchanging irritated looks on the other side. They don't like this; they don't like me being away from them, they don't like me keeping secrets. Who am I to argue? Jane knows my present, Anne knows my future. They know best, not from experience or wisdom, but from power.

We're stronger together, and no matter what happened today, I'll be weak if we're broken apart.

CHAPTER TEN

Lo

My sisters are mostly as I left them—the old ones still staring at nothing, the rest in clusters of three and four by the *Glasgow*, passing time slowly. Key is with the old ones, staring like they do, even though she is not truly old yet—she just wants to be, desperately. She's been talking about becoming an angel since the day we met and watches the old ones with reverence, admiration, like they've achieved something where she's failed. Molly is still by herself. *It's not natural for us to be alone before we're old*, I think, before realizing that I'm alone, too. And part of me wants to stay that way, but another part of me longs to join the others. . . . I've already forgotten a few of Naida's memories, though. . . . Maybe if I'm alone, I'll be able to hold on to more of them.

I slink around the ship, settle with my back against the exterior wall. Its name is written above me, almost faded entirely by the water. *Glasgow* isn't its full name—there are words that came before it, but all we can read is *of Glasgow*. I reach up, trace my fingers over the name on the slick wood. Just as I do so, a shadow flickers by me. I turn to see Molly passing, keeping her eyes firmly on her destination. There's more to Molly's name, too. I am still my sisters, they are me, but Molly and I are different. We both remember.... Maybe I could talk to her; we could tell each other our memories. Maybe she could help me hold on to mine, and I could help her hold on to hers.

I swim after her, around the hull, into the belly of the ship. I realize where she's going—one of the back bedrooms. She cuts down a hallway, around an overturned piece of furniture covered in seaweed. Walls, walls everywhere—she passes through a larger room adorned with a chandelier; light fingers its way in from a crack in the ceiling and makes the chandelier's glass cast tiny rainbows on the floor. I haven't been this far inside the *Glasgow* in ages. Molly disappears through a doorway, into the dark. I pause for a moment, follow—

Molly's face is in front of mine, eyes dark, sharp—I cry out in surprise. She looks less human than before, more like a sea creature whose home I've disturbed. She pushes toward me, forcing me to swim backward until my shoulder blades hit the remains of a picture frame on the wall behind me.

I remember...I remember a picture frame, the sort that you put things in. There was a white dress behind it, a baby's dress. My name was below. No, not my name, Naida's name. I squint my eyes shut, try to see more of the memory, the lace on the dress's sleeves, but it's gone almost immediately. I wish I could reach out for Celia, have her remind me—

"Why are you following me?" Molly bursts into the fading memory. Her words aren't hateful, actually, not even spiteful. They're irritated. Like I've interrupted something.

"I want to talk to you," I say slowly. "About the past."

Molly looks at me for a long time. Nothing softens, nothing welcomes me, nothing suggests this was even remotely a good idea.

"About my past?" she finally says.

"And mine."

Molly exhales, still steely-eyed. "My past is gone. I'll never get it back." She turns, retreats through the doorway. I slowly follow, peer into the room. There's a bed frame, the rusted springs of a mattress, a tipped-over lamp. I want seeing them to spur another memory in me, but they are nothing, just things in the water. Molly reaches out, wistfully touches a pile of something—shoes—clumped in the corner.

I swallow, speak. "Do you remember—"

"Yes. I remember everything," she hisses, and I can't tell if she's telling the truth or if the claim is just a desperate lie. "Everything I won't ever have again."

"You'll be happier if you forget," I tell her instantly, a well-rehearsed line, one we all say to the new girls. As it leaves my mouth, I wonder if it's true. Molly looks at me, blinks, stares hard. I regret saying anything, regret encouraging her to forget when suddenly I can't bear the thought of doing so.

"Everyone would be happier if they forgot," she says. "Humans, us, angels. Do you remember how we changed? Why we changed?"

I shake my head. "Nothing before the angel bringing us to the ocean, like everyone else."

Molly smiles a little, but it's cold. "Ah. The *angel*. Of course." The way she says it is dangerous. It's fine for the very, very new girls to question the idea of angels, but girls Molly's age should know better. We would never cast a girl out, of course, but doubting what happens after we grow old might as well be exile—none of us wants to talk to someone with doubts, none of us wants to be upset by someone's unproven ideas and lies. Even now, having remembered my name, Molly's tone makes me uncomfortable. She must see the concern on my face, because she pauses, then moves on quickly. "Well, I still remember what happened before that. Just barely. Why it was us instead of some other human girl, and how it all happened. It was terrible, you know."

"Tell me," I say, breathless.

She looks at me, shakes her head. "You said it yourself. You'll be happier if you forget. Everyone else is." Her words are daggerlike, and I feel my chest spark with frustration. I want to know. She has to tell me....

Molly rises, turns her back to me. She traces the top of the bed frame, lets her hand drift to where pillows might be if they hadn't long decayed. "Drowning the boy wouldn't have been so bad. It's a terrible way to die. But death is nothing compared with what happened to us."

I close my eyes as Molly settles in the spot between the shoes and the bed, pleased with herself. She remembers. We could have helped each other remember. She knows how we became ocean girls; she knows a part of my past that I don't.

I shake my head at Molly, back away. Past the picture frame, down the hall, back to where the water isn't still. When I reach the open ocean, I gasp, let the sweet electric feeling that links me and my sisters flow through and overwhelm me. *This is easier, so much easier than remembering,* I think as the ocean current swirls around me, supports me, loves me. So much easier than trying to remember a life that's been shattered into a million tiny memories, impossible to put back together.

But in the back of my mind, I hear Naida. I pity her. A girl I once was, a girl who I mourn.

I can't forget her now.

CHAPTER ELEVEN

❧

Celia

It's Wednesday, time for my triple date with Jude. Anne and Jane are giggly and ecstatic—they make me change clothes four times until I've achieved what they call "the perfect combination of heroine and girl-next-door," which apparently means my oldest jeans and one of Jane's ultragirly tops.

The Landing is a touristy shopping center with an alligator adventure park and a bunch of carts that sell things like airbrushed T-shirts and shot glasses with palmettos on them. That said, the Thai place here serves lunches cheap enough that we can afford them on the allowance our uncle gives us, especially when Anne and Jane are getting so many of our other expenses paid for by their conquests. We park near the back of the lot to avoid the sea of SUVs up front, bypass the long line for the ice-cream shop, and find seats on the Thai place's patio. The heat is bad, but we've always enjoyed watching yachts ease through the canals, imagining which one we'd like to own one day.

"Where is he?" Anne says, looking at her phone to check the time.

"We're early," I say. "He's always running late." He was even late to his stepfather's funeral, according to his memories, though that might have been intentional—I couldn't see it clearly.

"Celia!" Anne and Jane exchange puzzled glances, then we all look in the direction the voice came from. On the Landing's center strip, where the vendor carts are set up, is a much drier, happier version of Jude than the one I saw the other night. And he's wearing a hat with foam palm trees shooting out of it.

"Is that—" Anne begins.

"Oh my god, he's one of the cart people," Jane says, but she looks delighted anyway.

Jude, apparently, is manning a cart that sells annoyingly wacky hats—ones with dolphins, sea turtles, or beach balls shooting out of them. He pulls down the canvas sides of the cart, ties them up, and jogs toward us, lightly jumping over the railing that separates the patio from the sidewalk. As drowned and soggy as Jude looked in the hospital, he looks the opposite now. His hair is a mess, and he's wearing jeans and a plaid shirt with the sleeves rolled up; I can see the tattoos covering his arms disappear under the fabric. He arrives at our table, sweating from the heat and still wearing the palm-tree hat. I can't tell if Anne and Jane are entirely charmed or entirely horrified. He doesn't look at them, though; he stares at me, lips curled into a smile.

"Strange," he finally says. "I remembered you being brunette, not blond."

I try not to cringe as I think about Naida's chocolate-colored hair. So he *does* remember her.

"Then how did you know it was her?" Jane asks, voice flirty.

"I've been yelling 'Celia' every time I see a group of three girls. You're the first set that's turned around. I'm right, aren't I?" Jude says, grinning.

"Right. Hi," I finally say. Jude turns back to me and extends a hand. I let it hang awkwardly in the air for a moment before grimacing and shaking it. I stiffen as more memories hit me, this time details about his first love, his first kiss, the way the sunlight looked in her hair—

I release his palm. *Way* too much information in that memory . . .

"Sorry," he says. "I just feel like, you know, at least shake the hand of the person who saved your life."

"Sit down," Anne says, pointing to the chair beside me. He obliges, sweeping the palm-tree hat off as he does so.

"It's my uniform. No, seriously. My boss says that we sell more when we wear the palm-tree one."

"This is your job?" Jane says. "I thought you were a musician."

"Haven't you heard the whole 'starving artist' thing?" Jude asks. Jane nods. "It's true. Dr. Wacky's pays the bills. Or at

95

least some of the bills. The smaller ones, mostly." He leans back and fans himself with the menu—I can see more of his tattoos now. Flowers and waves on his lower right arm open up into an image of a mermaid on his upper. She's blue-skinned and blond, with a long, curled fishtail. She looks nothing like Naida, but it's not the tail or hair that makes them different— it's something to do with her mouth, her demure smile. It's an expression I can't imagine on Naida's lips.

"So," Jude says. "Sisters. Twins?" He motions to Anne and Jane.

"Triplets," Anne corrects him, and points back at me. "I'm Anne."

"Jane," she introduces herself.

"Is there a trick to telling the two of you apart?"

"No," Anne answers a little smugly.

"Damn," he says. The fact that *he* has no problem telling me apart from Anne and Jane doesn't bother me like it does with others.

We order cheap appetizers as our meal, all with silly beach-themed names like Krazy Kokonut Shrimp and Baha-marita Alligator Bites. It helps that there's also a bottomless basket of hush puppies, which is a standard for every restau-rant in town, even a Thai one. I jump every time Jane or Anne reaches for a hush puppy and it looks like they might touch Jude, try to read him. I already know so much about him; it isn't fair that they get to know even more. They behave, though, and I start to relax and actually listen to what Jude is saying. It's nothing I don't already know, pretty much—

96

where he's from, no siblings, lived here for two years—but I pretend for a little while that this is all new information, like we're normal people meeting and I don't have to act like I couldn't practically write an essay on his past.

I'm so relaxed, I guess, that I let my guard down by the end of the meal, which is exactly when Jane strikes. Reaching across the table for the last spring roll, she lets her hand brush Jude's arm. It's hardly anything, but it was enough, clearly, because I see Anne and Jane exchange glances. I sigh. What's the point in trying?

Jane giggles quietly over whatever she saw. When Jude gets up to go pay at the register a few minutes later, she loses it, dissolving into a fit of laughter.

"Stop it," I beg her, straight-faced. "Don't mess with him like the others."

"What did you see?" Anne asks excitedly.

"No! He's nice. Don't do this!"

"Oh, he may be nice," Jane says, holding up her hands. "But just so you know, Celia, he was thinking about you naked when I touched him. He has...what's it called, when you save someone and they fall for you?"

"Oh, I know this. Nightingale syndrome? Like Florence Nightingale? Or am I making that up? I hate history class," Anne says, ignoring the fact that I'm blushing furiously. It's not that I even care if Jude thought about me naked—okay, I care a little, but that's not the point. I don't think I'm the one he's fallen for, if he's fallen for anyone. He remembers Naida, not me. He's just confused.

97

"Stop it! Both of you, stop!" I finally snap, though I'm talking to my subconscious as much as my sisters. Their eyes widen at my tone—I never talk to them this way. We never talk to *one another* this way. I'm instantly sorry, but not sorry enough to say so aloud. My sisters fall silent for a few heartbeats, giving Jude just enough time to return.

"So, where are you three headed now? And is it somewhere that a fine animal-shaped hat might be appreciated?" he asks. "Because I've got a stingray hat back at the cart that would look lovely on you, Anne. Or are you Jane?"

"Jane has to go get her hair cut after this," Anne answers, irritation with me lacing her voice. "After that we're just going home. I think we're going out tonight."

"All three of you?" Jude asks.

"I'm not," I cut in. *I can be just as bitter as you, Anne.*

"Ah," Jude says, becoming aware that he's touched on something uncomfortable. He glances from Anne to me, then speaks slowly. "You know, Celia . . . you said to tell you if there was anything you could do to help me earn guitar-fund money. What if I were to call in that favor this afternoon? I mean, if you really don't have any plans."

"How will I get home?" I ask.

"I've got a car," Jude says. "I'll take you."

I nod at Jude; Anne rolls her eyes at both of us. "Fine. Nice meeting you, Jude. We've got to get back. We'll see you later tonight, Celia?"

"Sure," I say through a sigh. Anne rises, drops her napkin

on the table, and starts out. Jane follows suit, grinning at Jude before she hurries off.

Jude and I are silent for a moment. A long moment.

"So... did I just miss something?" he finally says, turning to me.

"Kind of," I answer. "They don't like it when I disagree with them. They really don't like it when I'm vocal about it."

"And did I hear one of them say I have Florence Nightingale syndrome?"

Of all the things he could have heard, I actually think that's the least embarrassing. I shrug my shoulders and nod.

"Interesting," he says, screwing up his eyebrows for a moment. "Would it help if I told you I don't?"

"Not really."

"What about if I told you that I'm not a stalker or anything weird?"

"Not convincing, seeing how you found my cell number Saturday night."

Jude sucks in air through his teeth. "Hm. That does look bad, doesn't it? Maybe I do have Nightingale syndrome. Sorry about that."

"Don't worry about it. And you *don't* have it," I say, shaking my head at him, trying not to picture Naida leaning over him that night. We rise, and I follow Jude back to the Dr. Wacky's cart, where he rolls up the canvas and situates the palm-tree hat back on his head firmly.

"Here. Pick one," he says, motioning to the cart.

"What? Why do I have to wear one?"

"Because you said you'd do me a favor. And also so I'm not the only one that looks like a moron wearing a foam hat," he says, grinning, which is why fifteen minutes later, amid a trickling stream of customers, I'm wearing a hat with sea turtles on it. When I move my head, their flippers wiggle.

"Tell me something," Jude says. "About you, I mean. Because basically, all I know is you have two sisters, you prefer sea turtles to stingrays, and you sometimes save people from drowning."

I smile, wrap my ankles around the legs of the stool I'm sitting on. "I..." I can't think of anything to say. I like history class? I like the ocean? I hate cheap chocolate? Everything about me seems to be so caught up in my sisters and our powers, I can't think of anything to share with a stranger. For a moment I find myself wishing he could see my past, if only so he'd understand my silence.

Jude looks a little amused, but nods. "All right...what about this—I'll tell you trivia about me, but you have to tell me matching trivia about you."

"Like what?"

"Like...here, trivia: In third grade I had to do this report on Indians. I worked really hard and made this poster and had a costume and everything. And after the report was over, I found out that my teacher meant 'Indians' as in 'India,' not 'Indians' as in 'Native Americans.'"

I nod, grin—I didn't know that memory. "Okay, okay.

In...fifth grade, I think—maybe sixth—Anne, Jane, and I used to try to switch places in classes."

"Did it work?"

"For them it did. But anyone who knew us at all could always tell it was me. I spent a lot of that year in detention for it," I admit.

For an hour, things are different. I didn't know as much about Jude as I'd thought—I mean, yes, I knew the big picture, but there are so many details, so many little things I didn't see, that I wouldn't know if we weren't playing the trivia game. Sweat trickles down my neck despite the umbrella shading us and the waters we buy from a passing cart.

"Seriously, it used to infuriate me," I say. "They called me Mother Celia for, like...a year."

"All because you were named after your mother? I think they're jealous."

"Anne and Jane don't get jealous," I say. "But...I do like that I have my mother's name."

"You were close with her?"

"Not at all, I barely knew her. But she was exciting and beautiful, and everyone adored her. She and my father had this dramatic love story; she was a rich girl from the city and he was a poor woodsman, but she ran away with him anyway." I can feel myself grinning as I tell the story. "She said her life started that day."

"That *is* dramatic," Jude says, nodding. "Are you like her, at least?"

I exhale. "Not really." I hesitate. "Or maybe just not *yet*."

"An optimist," Jude says, smiling. "All right, all right. Let's see...to match that...I've got an excellent one. But you'll owe me like...fifty pieces of trivia about yourself if I tell you." He inhales deeply, closes his eyes. "My name isn't Jude."

I hesitate—I probably look more shocked than is fitting. But in all the memories I saw, I never heard someone call him another name. Were the memories wrong? Did I read them incorrectly? I run through them in my head, alarmed.

"Relax, it's not *that* bad a name...." Jude says, a little concerned. I try to wipe my expression away.

"What is it, then?" I ask.

"Well, first off, it's a family name. It's tradition—every first son gets stuck with it. So in middle school, I renamed myself after the Beatles song. You know it?"

"*Hey Jude*? Of course."

"Oh, good, I don't have to start hating you. Anyway, it didn't really stick until I moved away from home. Only my roommates know the truth, and that's only because my rent checks still say Barnaby."

I try to smash the smile spreading across my face but can't help it. I laugh, and Jude's ears turn pink. He rolls his eyes while I get the humor out but smiles a little himself at the same time.

"I know, I know. Everyone in third grade thought it was a riot, too. You see why I changed it? No one would give money to a musician named Barnaby. What about you? Do you play any instruments? Create any art?"

"Not really. I took a painting class at Milton's once; we made watercolor flowers for nine weeks. No music, though. There's only a choir program there, and I definitely *don't* sing."

Jude pauses, looking a little confused. "Really? I remember you singing on the beach."

I stumble a little but shake my head. "Nope. I don't sing."

"Huh. I could have sworn you did. What *do* you do, then, other than hang out with your sisters?"

"I...nothing," I answer. "Nothing. Really. I go to school, I get decent grades, I...I guess in some ways, being Anne's and Jane's sister is really all I have time to be. Or energy, at least."

Jude raises an eyebrow. "Poetic. Though it'd be more so if you weren't wearing a hat covered in sea turtles."

I laugh. "I know, it's not very exciting."

"I think you do more than that," Jude says. "Maybe you just don't realize it yet. Like, for example, might I remind you that you save drowning victims and give them terrible cases of Nightingale syndrome. That's pretty exciting."

"You don't have Nightingale syndrome," I say.

"I could!"

"Yeah, yeah. Your turn."

"Okay..." Jude says, inhaling. "I...I left home because my mom lied to me about half a pie."

"A pie?"

"Half a pie," he corrects, grinning. "She said we were out of this pie I brought home from food day in French class.

Really, she'd hidden it so she could eat the whole thing herself."

"And pie hoarding made you head to the beach?" I ask.

"Well, technically, yes," he says, adjusting his hat. "Not really, though. Really...I realized that she was always lying to me. She lied to me about why my dad left, about my step-father being great, about a thousand little things every day. I was sick of the lies." He looks up at me, smiles a little. "Sorry. Too much information."

"No," I say, shaking my head. "I didn't know that's why you left. I knew she lied a lot, but I thought—"

"You knew she lied?" Jude asks, confused. "How?"

Damn it. "You said it earlier, I think, maybe," I say, trying to brush it off. "But it wasn't too much information."

"Good...good," Jude says, still looking confused. I curse at myself when he looks away. "But yeah. That's why I'm here. That's why I hate lying."

I grimace. Fantastic—he hates lying, and I'm practically a professional liar between keeping Naida and my power secret. Jude continues. "What about you? How'd you get here?"

I inhale—at least this I can be honest about. "My father has Alzheimer's, so he can't take care of us. Our mother is gone. Our brothers are spread across the country, and we hardly know them. All I have are my sisters. We've been at Milton's for seven years."

"Wow. No wonder they're protective of you."

"Protective? More like...stifling."

Jude laughs. "That, too."

Another moment of silence. Jude drums his fingers on the register, then grins. "Okay, I've got one. So, when I was a little kid, I loved pop music...."

I knew that. I know the story he's about to tell me.

But this time, for the first time, that's okay.

CHAPTER TWELVE

Lo

When it rains, it's beautiful under the water. It's like the sky and the ocean and the clouds are all connected as we lie on the deck of the *Glasgow* and stare up at the waves that rock far above us. They look dangerous even in a small rainstorm like this. They look beautiful. They remind us that the ocean isn't something we've tamed, just because we're a part of it.

Key and I used to play a game; when it stormed, we'd inch toward the surface, each daring the other to go a little higher, a little higher—nowhere near the actual breaking point, of course, but we'd get just close enough that the waves pulled us back and forth and the rolls of thunder ripped through our chests. It was dangerous; in a storm, you have to fight so hard against the water that sometimes you'll lose yourself in the process, and either instantly grow old or simply be killed by the waves. But Key and I were rebels, wild things, and we dared to challenge the weather—at least, until I got frightened. Then I'd run back down to the seafloor and she'd follow, having always won, gone a little bit higher than me. I look over and realize Key is looking at me, smiling, like we're both just sharing the same memory. Why haven't we done that in ages? Hurricane season will be starting soon—hurricanes often sweep away many of the old ones at once, take them to the surface to transform....

I should be going to the surface now. I said I'd meet Celia tonight.

I slip away from the others, down around the back side of the ship. There, I curl my fingers into the seaweed for a moment, like it can give me strength, then shoot to the surface quickly, grimacing the whole way. When I emerge by the shore, I realize. The storm lost most of its power out at sea; there's only the slightest pattering of rain on the ocean's surface. The wind is still sharp, though; I wince and dip so low in the water that only my eyes are showing. They've fixed the pier, I notice, looking ahead. I remember for a moment the boy falling, Molly's eyes lighting up....

Celia is here—by the church, the same place we sat last time. Her skin matches the color of the few bits of sky peeking through the rain clouds, where the sun is setting—peach and red, colors I hardly ever see down deep. I look up—there are people on the pier above me. How far into the slowly darkening distance can they see? I dive down and move along underneath the pier, dodging old fishing lines and lures. When the water is waist-deep, I inhale. I have to stand, I have to stand. . . . As hard as it is to remember Naida, it's so, so easy to remember the pain of walking.

"Wait!" I look up at the shore. Celia is standing in the darkness at the pier's edge, balancing on rocks. "I thought these might help?" She holds up a pair of shoes, the strappy kind humans wear when they walk along the shore. It's almost comical, to think of myself wearing them, but I'll try anything to stop the pain. I nod, and she tosses them to me, grimacing when they go off course and the ocean takes hold. I slink back through the water and find them, a speck of bright purple against the thrashing waters. When I put them on, they feel strange, uncomfortable. They drag in the water and slow me down. But I finally go back to the shore, near Celia. I wince, putting one shoed foot firmly down on the sand.

The pain is intense, terrible—just like before, the knives shoot through the softest parts of my feet and scrape along my bones. I tremble . . . but when I look down, there's less blood. That's something, at least. My legs are shaky as I walk the rest of the way out, trying not to shout so loudly that the people on the pier above hear me. When I reach the shore, I drop down to the sand by Celia to let my feet rest.

"I also . . . I brought you this?" Celia says, sounding embarrassed. I look up, pushing my hair from my eyes—why can't it stay out of my face like it does underwater?—and see she's holding a dress. It's old, the fabric weathered and washed. It's so dry. I watch drops of ocean water splash it, blossom into thick wet spots.

"Why?" I don't understand—the shoes made sense, sort of, but a dress?

"Because . . . you're naked? Last time, you wanted a towel?"

I hesitate, look out over the water. For a moment, I get lost, wondering what my sisters are doing beneath the waves. . . .

"I wanted it?" I ask, turning back to her.

She nods. "You don't have to. I just thought, if someone were to see you, they might think . . ."

"Of course," I say. "Right." I take the dress from her hands and struggle to slide it over my head. It feels strange on my skin, uncomfortable, like it'll hold me back from moving all the ways I want to. I'm certain I don't look like Celia in it, that I just look like an ocean girl in a dress, every bit as awkward as it would look on a dolphin or a fish.

I suppose it's something, though. Celia rises and walks away, back toward the church. I follow, stumbling a little against the searing pain in my feet, longing for the moment we sit down. If the people on the pier think anything is strange about me, they don't show it—their eyes skim over Celia and me, instead staring out at the ocean, to where the stars are starting to shine. It looks odd from here. When you're in the middle of the ocean, the stars are everywhere when you look up. But here, I see them stop, the dark line where the water begins and the sky ends. I stare at the horizon for a moment when we finally sit by the church.

"I saw Jude today," Celia says awkwardly, drumming on her knees. "The boy from the water, the one you saved?"

"Oh." Jude. He has a name. Naturally he has a name, but for some reason I always just thought of his eyes, not the name, the mind, the life behind them. "He's alive?" I can't pretend it isn't a relief to hear.

"Yes. He . . . he remembers you, I think," she says, looking away.

"What does he remember?"

"Your hair. And . . . did you sing to him?"

I pause. "No. Another one of us did, though." Celia still looks confused, but I'm not sure I could phrase an explanation in a way she could understand. She couldn't possibly understand what it's like to be one of us.

"Well . . . he's nice. He's really nice," Celia says, words a little stilted. I look at her, at the expression on her face—it's different, tried.

"Does he love you?" I ask.

Celia's eyebrows shoot up. She stumbles over the beginnings of several sentences before landing on one. "No, of course not. We just met. And he . . . it's just that he thinks I saved him, which he shouldn't, because it was you. . . ." Her face turns red with something like guilt.

"But he might love you?" I ask, ignoring the rest of what she's said.

Celia seems surprised. "I . . . no. My sisters say he does, but that's just because they don't know what love is. They think it's a game. . . ." She drifts off, sounding embarrassed. We're silent for a few minutes, listening to the ocean. She moves a lot, I notice, brushing her hair back, flitting her eyes

110

across the water, like the tiny fish that stay near the shore. "Are you...right now, what's your name?" Celia asks, like she's confused.

"Lo," I whisper. Lo, the ocean girl, the girl who can't be loved. I open my eyes, tilt my head toward her. "I want to remember Naida."

"That's why I came," she answers. She inhales, looks at her hand, eyes softening like she's praying. Then she slowly, carefully places her fingers over my forearm.

I can feel Celia in my mind, almost. I try to understand what she's looking for. She suddenly grips my arm tighter; I flinch as her fingers dig into my skin.

Something in me moves, changes. It's like a wall in my head is crumbling. I inhale, realize I've been holding my breath. Tiny bits of memories swarm me—trees, light, silverware, rocking chairs, little things—I can't hold on to them long enough, I need help. I look up at Celia, who pulls her hand away and smiles at me shakily.

"There was a rope swing in your backyard, tied to a tree. Do you remember?" she asks.

My lips part, a soft sound escapes them.

"Yes..."

CHAPTER THIRTEEN

Naida

I picture the swing, the honeysuckle vines that grew up one side, then turn to Celia. "Do your sisters think you're with Jude right now?" I ask. Everything feels light and perfect, like the weight of billions of drops of water has been hoisted from my mind, and that asking about Jude, living a little vicariously through Celia, will remove the tiny weight that remains.

She smiles, looks almost relieved by my question. "I think they do. I told them I was going for a walk alone, but they weren't buying it. Oh well. It'll mess with their heads, drive them crazy...." She smiles but sighs a little.

"Are they both older than you, then?"

"Technically they are, by a few minutes. We're triplets."

"My sister was three years older," I say, leaning my head back against the church. I close my eyes, inhale, and words emerge from my mouth as easily as if I were reading a book aloud. "She was the smart one, the pretty one, the perfect one. It was like no matter what I did, I wasn't her." I stop, inhale. How did I know all that? I look at Celia, who smiles as thunder rolls overhead—a storm is sweeping in from farther out in the ocean.

"You remembered that on your own," she says.

"How, though?"

"The memories are still there, just buried. And I haven't seen much of your sister in your memories, so I know I didn't tell you any of that. Maybe talking like this triggers them, forces them out of hiding."

I pause, my lips part, I search for the book in my mind, the hidden recess where my old life lurks—I find it easier than the last time I met with Celia. "She...she had long brown hair, and she used this vanilla body wash, and we had to share this little room with a triangle ceiling that got hot in the summer. And her name—" I stop suddenly, like someone slammed a door shut in my head. The name is right there on the other side, but I can't grab it—

"It'll come," Celia says gently. "And if talking doesn't work, I can always try to read them for you."

I swallow hard, over the thickness in my throat—how can I not remember her name? Thunder again—a few drops start to fall. I watch the way they splash against my skin. I see Celia jump when lightning cracks through the clouds above.

"Come on," Celia says, and grabs the door of the church. It sticks, so she yanks harder—paint flutters off the frame when it finally gives. I follow her inside, turning back to look at the trail of blood I've left from the door. She props the door open, then sits down just inside the entryway. I take a seat beside her, sigh as the pressure against my feet is relieved. The back of the church is filled with pews that are tossed together like toys, the ground is dusted with sand and dried sea grass, and it smells of the salt I'm sure the wooden floor has absorbed. As the wind picks up, the walls creak and the light fixture over the pulpit sways, but we're dry—at least we're dry. Celia looks at me a little nervously as I stare at the waves chewing at the shore.

"I don't know what changed. Do you?" Celia asks. I turn to look at her, and she continues, face in shadow. "Why you're like this now? How you can live in the water?"

I shake my head. "All I remembered before I met you was a man bringing me to the water, showing me how to find the other girls, but at that point I was already different, I wasn't really like you anymore. And the water..." I look back to the waves, and the sound of the thunderstorm pounding on the roof intensifies. "I'm not sure. Right now it seems crazy that I'd come out of or go back into it. But then when I'm there, it makes sense." I smile a little, though it feels fake. "As much sense as a girl who can read your past does, anyway."

"Fair point," Celia says. "I was just wondering... maybe that scream in your head... maybe the reason it's clouding everything is it was the change. I think the screaming happened when Lo was created. Do you remember who the man was? Maybe he knows what changed before he helped you."

I feel Lo thumping in my head as I answer. "I don't know his name. They say he was an angel. That he'll come back for us when we grow old."

There's a long pause. Lightning crashes somewhere outside, barely audible over the roar of the waves. Celia looks at me strangely. "Naida. You're Naida right now, aren't you?"

"I think so. Yes. But Lo is always there. And I'm always here when Lo is...here. It's like I'm asleep and dreaming about Lo's life, and then I wake up and I'm me again."

She waits a long time before speaking. "Do you remember anything about the man who brought you here? Maybe I can find him."

I close my eyes, try to think back. "Scars," I say. "He had scars on his chest, thick ones. But that's all I remember."

"Then why do you—why does *Lo* believe he's an angel?" she asks.

I pause, smile a little at how stupid my words are going to sound. "Why do you believe in angels here on shore? Because they have to, I guess. They have to believe in something, or it means we're all just sea foam when it's over—" No, no. That's Lo talking, winding her way back into my head. I close my eyes, smother her voice.

"That's true," Celia says, apparently not noticing Lo's

voice interrupting mine—a fact that bothers me. "But I haven't seen anything like angels in your memories."

"He didn't have wings...." I explain slowly. This memory is half Lo's, and it's hard to see, but I don't dare let her rise back up to give a full answer. "He didn't look anything like an angel, I don't think. But whatever happened with the screaming, he made the pain go away when he brought me here." I turn to her. "Is it that horrible? The screaming?"

Celia inhales. "Yes. It scared me, the first time I touched you."

"You can stop. If you need to," I say, but I can't look at her as I do.

"No," Celia says swiftly, and then, as if to convince herself, "No. I want to help. You're the first person I've been able to help with my power."

"Are your sisters like you?" I ask. "Can they read the past?"

Celia pauses, long enough that I can tell she's debating something important. "No. They have other...talents."

"But you don't want to tell me what those are," I say.

She shakes her head. "They're not mine to tell."

I nod. "It's good that you don't tell me. They're your sisters, they're important. You only get so many." I only had one. One, and I can't remember her name. I have others now, under the water, but it's not the same, is it? Down there, it feels like they're as good as blood, but now, they're nothing more than fellow victims of some mysterious, scream-inducing force. "You should tell them about me, though. Don't keep secrets."

"They'd never believe me," she says, laughing a little.

I drag my toe along the wooden floor, leaving a crescent shape in the sand. Would I tell my sister something like this, if I could remember her name?

If I could remember *anything* about her? I shake off the misery that's ebbing around my mind.

"Keep talking," I say. "Maybe we can trigger another memory."

CHAPTER FOURTEEN

Lo

Are we not good enough?
A night or two later, that's all I think over and over and over. Aren't my sisters good enough? I think about my past as a human, my future as an angel, like they're two great lights and I'm currently in darkness. But I'm happy with my sisters. I love my sisters. Aren't they good enough for me? I should stay away from the shore, stay away from Naida. When Naida is talking to Celia, when she's in the forefront of our shared mind, I feel weak, dizzy. I ache to return to the water— she resists me more and more each time, till the pain is so intense I almost can't bear it. And yet...I want to remember her. I want her to remember her life. I want us to...I want to stop feeling like *us*, start feeling like one girl, with a past as Naida and a present as Lo.

To do that, I have to be able to surface as Lo. Stay myself instead of letting Naida take over every time. I grimace and push off the ocean floor, swimming diagonally in the direction of the pier.

I break the surface of the water swiftly just after crossing the sandbar. I punch out of the waves so hard that water splashes in a halo around my body. The wind sweeps around me. It hurts, it hurts badly; the water lapping around my shoulders is sweet relief in comparison. I wait for the memories to come back as the wind whistles around my ears.

Nothing.

Nothing at all. I rise a little farther out of the water, but it doesn't help. The pier is empty—it's late, I can tell by the tide. I look at the church ahead. Maybe if I go there...

At night, you can't see the red of the blood in the water, but I can feel it. It's warm compared with the waves, a slicker liquid. The shoes Celia gave me will help, but I have to make it to the church first. The tide isn't entirely out, but it's still a long distance. I squeeze my eyes shut and run.

Swords shoot through my heels, lodge themselves in my legs, stick into my knees. I collapse in front of the church, let tears flow for a few moments while I watch the white sand by my feet absorb the blood. It looks black in the moonlight, thick like the oil boats sometimes leave behind in the water. I reach into the church and pull out the shoes, the dress. Recreate everything just like it was before, try to remember. The shoes hurt my sliced feet, and the dress clings to the water on my skin. I don't remember it feeling this strange before, I don't remember it hurting so badly. I look over to where Celia was sitting, remember what she said. What color was the dog?

Nothing. Nothing at all. I can't even remember how big the dog was now. I only remember the dog existed because I *can't* remember what it looked like.

I can't do this alone. I try to stifle the tears that flow faster now, pull my knees to my chest and try to ignore the throbbing in my feet. It would have been easier if I'd never come back. If I'd let Naida go. Even if I remember the dog, I won't have a soul. I won't have my old life. I won't ever be Naida again.

"Are you all right?"

I jump—or rather, I jump the way I would if I were in the water. When there's air where the ocean should be, I tumble to the side and fall into the sand. I hear the voice calling to me, but all I can think about is how clumsy I am here, how it's hard to move when the space around you can't hold you up like the ocean does. I finally lie still, panting, feet aching from pressing into the ground as I tried to escape.

"Relax, I'm sorry, I didn't mean to scare you," the voice says. A male voice, I realize. I turn around to look.

The moon catches on the boy's cheekbones, his shoulders, his chest, but can't quite make it to his eyes. He's holding his hands up so I can see them; the left is dotted in calluses along the tip of each finger, like Molly's.

"I'm fine," I say. My voice sounds garbled. I sit up, try to act normal, even though I want so badly to run for the waves and dive deep. I can't let him see that, though; I have to wait till he leaves....

"Do I know you?" he asks, voice rising a little.

"No."

"Are you sure? You look familiar," he says. He doesn't sound certain; he sounds hopeful. Like he wants me to say yes but knows I won't. He kneels in the sand, keeping his hands where I can see them. The new angle means the moonlight just catches his eyes—yes.

I know him. And he knows me, in a way.

"My name's Jude," he says slowly. "Maybe you just have a familiar face."

Jude, the boy I saved. The boy Molly sang to, but the boy I pulled from the waves. He's looking at me intently, the same way he looked at me when he was in Molly's arms. Like he needs me, like I can save him even though we're not in the water anymore.

Jude, the boy Celia loves, even if she doesn't realize it yet. Jealousy flares up in me, but I force it down.

"Are you sure you're okay?" he asks again.

"I'm fine. You just startled me," I answer swiftly. I try to make my voice sound like Celia's, but it doesn't work—I still sound like the other ocean girls, almost like I'm speaking a different language than Jude is.

"It's almost one in the morning. I can understand not expecting someone," Jude agrees, nodding. "You're crying, though. You're not about to run into the ocean and end it all, are you?"

I laugh at the truth behind his statement, though I doubt he'd recognize the expression as laughter. "No," I answer. "I just came here to...think."

"So did I," he says, leaning back against the church. "I almost drowned here. I'm trying to get over it."

"Are you afraid of the water?" I ask, looking at him. He's staring out at the black waves, eyes intense.

"Yes," he admits. "I was always sort of afraid of it, though. I can't really swim, and then I fell off the pier. . . . It was horrible. I needed to breathe, and there was nothing, just more water. I felt myself dying—" He stops short. "Sorry, person-I-just-met-whose-name-I-don't-even-know. Yes. I'm afraid of the water."

"It's nothing to be afraid of," I say fondly. "You just have to remember that it doesn't care. It doesn't want to kill you, but it doesn't love you, either. That makes it dangerous, but it also makes it reliable. You can trust the ocean because it's always the same."

"That was beautiful. Like a song," Jude says, looking a little surprised. "I wish I had my guitar—it's at the bottom of the ocean somewhere, since I was wearing it when I fell."

"You can't get another?"

"I can," he says, "but I'd had that one for ages. Every song I've ever written, I wrote on it."

We wait a long time in the silence. I keep waiting for him to notice that my skin's the wrong color, that I look strange, but it's so dark that I guess he thinks it's just the moonlight. He thinks I'm human. The idea makes something burn in my chest, a light that spirals up through my heart.

He sighs. "Anyway, I'll leave you alone," he says, smiling at me. He starts to rise.

122

"You don't have to," I say quickly. "You weren't bothering me."

He stops, pauses for a few beats, then lowers himself back into the sand. "Can I know your name, then, if we're going to be late-night beach partners?"

"Lo." I say it fast, easily—should I have said Naida?

"Lo. Nice to meet you." I like the way it sounds when he says my name.

And then it's quiet again. I can tell he wants to ask why I'm crying, what I'm doing here, where I came from, but he doesn't. He sits, staring at the water, his hands, the water again. I want to answer the questions he isn't asking, but I can't. I can't tell him about my sisters, I can't tell him what I am. But even though I want to answer him, I also don't want to reveal the truth. He thinks I'm human, and I can't bear the thought of changing that.

"I haven't written anything since the accident," he says, fast, like he had to spit the words out. "I used to have this rule for myself, that I wrote a song every day. But ever since I fell, I haven't been inspired. Well, until just now, when you said that about the ocean." He looks at me, guilty almost, like he feels bad for confessing that. I look away, out over the water.

"I sing," I say quietly. "Or, I do now, anyhow."

"What types of songs?"

"Love songs, mostly," I say. "The sad kind."

"The best kind," Jude says, smiling a little. "When I was in the water, I remember someone singing to me. The nurse at the hospital tried to convince me it was an angel."

123

"It wasn't," I say.

"How do you know?"

I smile a tiny bit. "Because angels can't live underwater."

"Then how did I survive?" he asks. He's teasing me, joking with me. It feels strange. His voice is so different from mine; it varies with each word, each letter. Mine is always the same.

I would like to tell this boy that I saved him. I'd like to tell him I'm the angel, that I stopped Molly, that it was her singing but that it was deadly. I even want to tell him that I pulled him out before Celia even got involved. Would he joke with me and laugh the way Celia says he does? Would he be able to love me?

Something shoots up in my chest, something hungry, something starving. If he loves me, I could . . .

I'd be Naida again. For the first time, that bothers me— Naida doesn't feel sparked when Jude looks at her; Naida isn't the one who pulled him out of the water. *I* am. But his soul, if I persuaded him to want me . . . the ocean is so close. It'd be easy to pull him in. Naida would get her soul back, Lo would be . . . gone, I guess. But there'd be no more floating along, pulled by the water, forced into the air, unable to control any of it. Naida could go back to her old life, make her own decisions, be her own person. . . .

Would she forget me, the same way I've forgotten her?

Jude speaks, startling me. "I shouldn't say all that. I survived because this girl pulled me out of the water and gave me CPR. Maybe she *is* the angel."

124

Celia. "Maybe," I answer.

"I keep thinking about her. Her sisters think it's just because she saved me, and maybe they're right, but I just—"

"I have to go," I interrupt. I have to go. Part of me— Naida, I guess—wants this boy's soul, part of me wants the boy, and all of me knows this is wrong. He's Celia's. He's innocent.

He's human.

Jude hurries to his feet, and before I can stop him, he leans down and offers me a hand.

"I'll..." I don't know what to say. I don't want to stand in front of him for fear he'll see how it hurts me. But I can't just not take his hand. I exhale and slide my fingers into his. He pulls me to standing, then lets go.

The knives are boring into me, twisting, tearing the bones on the top of my feet; it feels like they might break apart like pieces of driftwood. I don't wince. I can't, I can't cry; he'll know. Instead I stare at him, unwilling to move, unable to move. He's looking at me closely. I worry for a moment he'll realize I look wrong, even in the moonlight.

"It was nice meeting you," he says. "I hope you find whatever it is you're looking for out here."

"So do I," I say. I inhale. He's waiting for me to move.

I'll have to walk. I'll have to pretend like it doesn't hurt. He thinks I'm a human girl, and not only should I not let that stop...I don't *want* it to stop. I inhale, turn. One foot in front of the other. Step, another step, another. I feel blood drip from the shoes, hope that the moonlight hides any trace

125

of it in the sand. Another, another. Just get far enough into the dark, then I can dive, go back to where there's no pain... Is this what the fish, the dolphins, the whales feel like when they find themselves trapped on the shore?

I glance back at him; he's still watching me. I wave, he waves back, then turns to leave. I think about him under the water, the way his limbs flailed around his body, the way he couldn't live beneath the waves the way we so easily do.

Another step. Another. Burning through my legs, it feels like my toes are being severed.

Into the dark, into the water—I hit my knees and let the ocean rush around me, soothe my feet, calm me like a friend with each wave that laps against my legs. When I pulled him out, I didn't know what I was getting into. I didn't know Celia could do the things she does. I didn't even know I was Naida.

I didn't know how much it could hurt to be Lo.

CHAPTER FIFTEEN

✸

Celia

"Where have you been the last few nights?" Anne asks several days later at a café down the street from the dorms. This area is unabashedly antitourist; there are no beach towels, no inflatable alligators, no neon signs. It's tucked away neatly behind the school, and were it not for the salt in the air, it could very well pass for a street in the middle of the country instead of at its edge. I stall, tapping the bottom of a mustard bottle to drown the order of fries we're sharing—a taste all three of us love and just about everyone else seems to hate.

The silence goes on a beat too long, long enough that I can practically feel Anne growing suspicious. "I've been hanging out with someone I met here, when Jude fell off the pier."

"Hanging out? Like, a friend?" Jane says, furrowing her brows. The way she says *friend* is odd—not only because the three of us don't really have friends, so to speak, but because

I'm not sure I really consider Naida a friend. She's more like…a cause. I barely know her. But then, I like her. *Friend* isn't a crazy term, I guess.…I nod at Jane.

"Who is it?" Anne asks.

"Her name's Naida," I say.

"A girl?" Jane asks in disbelief.

"We were friends with that girl, the younger sister, in Ellison," I argue.

"For all of five minutes," Anne says. "But forget it—who is she?" They sound like they think she might be a spy from another set of triplets.

The lie is on the edge of my lips, ready to go: a girl from the public school. Just someone to hang out with. It's nothing, really. Don't worry.

But I think of Naida, of the sister she can't remember. *You only get so many.*

These are mine. They're my sisters. It's my power, it should be my choice and mine alone…even if we are stronger together. I inhale. "She has trouble remembering things. I'm helping her."

Anne's and Jane's eyes widen. They look at each other. "She knows what you can do?" There's a note of panic in Anne's voice, fear, even.

"It's fine," I say swiftly, shaking my head. "She doesn't remember anything from before a few years ago, and I touched her and…it's not what you think, Anne. I promise, it's fine." Revealing that Naida knows about the power is one thing; that she's something like a mermaid is another thing entirely.

128

"Did you tell her about Jane and me?" Anne says, voice low. I hesitate, wishing I hadn't said anything. The secret was bad, but the look on Anne's face is worse, as is what she's said—*Jane and me*. Like the space between my sisters and me is much larger than a restaurant table.

"No," I answer. "Well, I told her I had sisters. But I didn't tell her about the powers—"

"We don't tell people, Celia. We've never told people," Anne hisses. "How could you?"

"I'm helping her. She needs me. You have to trust me, please. She's fine. She can't tell anyone."

"Yes, she can—"

"No. She really can't." I breathe in as the waitress stops by to refill our drinks; I think she realizes she's interrupted something, because she scurries away quickly when she's done. I continue, "If you're that worried, Jane can look. She can see I'm not lying."

Of course, if Jane looks, she'll know what Naida is, where she comes from—if I let Jane in to see details, she'd inevitably see the core as well. But I'm counting on Anne balking at the very suggestion that Jane essentially use her power against me. Use her power because they don't trust me. Even if it's true, it isn't something Anne would want to admit.

Anne presses her lips together. "It's fine," she says swiftly. "If you say it's fine, it's fine."

Her words are stilted—caught between saying what she wants to believe is true and what she's scared isn't. To be honest, I'm impressed. Anne is so used to being in control. Handing the reins to me is clearly uncomfortable, but she tries to manage it nonetheless. For that much, at least, I'm grateful.

"I promise. It's fine," I tell both of them sincerely.

"Can we meet her?" Jane asks.

My phone rings right as the last syllable is off Jane's tongue; I'm relieved to see Jude's number pop up and save me from answering Jane's question. How could I introduce Naida to my sisters? How could I explain her?

"Good news," Jude says the moment I answer. "I'm going to buy a new guitar today."

"That's . . . good," I say back, a little perplexed.

"You should come with me."

"Why?"

"Because you're involved now. You shouldn't have saved me if you didn't want to end up hanging out with me. This is entirely your fault."

I pause for a long time.

Jude ups the offer. "And we can go get ice cream, if you want?"

I laugh, and Jude offers to pick me up at the café, then we hang up. Jane takes the easy bait, immediately asking about where Jude and I are going, what we're doing, how long I'll be gone, do I want to run home and borrow her new shirt. Anne isn't as quick to forget about Naida, though; I can see her thinking carefully, choosing her words. She doesn't speak until Jude's car rumbles into the parking lot.

"Eventually we'll get to meet her, right?" It isn't really a question, not the way Anne's asking it.

"Of course," I lie swiftly, standing up and collecting my purse.

"Right," Anne says, and I can tell she knows I'm lying. "Well, don't do that again, Celia, telling people about us."

"I didn't tell her about us. I told her about *me*."

"Same thing," Anne says, like this should have been obvious. I shrug like Jane does when Anne's irritated with her and turn, relieved when I push through the glass café door. Jude turns down some sort of bluesy music as I arrive and fall into the car's front seat.

"Is Anne glaring at me? I think she's glaring at me," he says, nodding toward Anne and Jane in the café window.

"You can tell them apart?" I ask, impressed.

"Of course. Anne is the one who always looks like she might murder me."

I laugh as Jude backs out of the parking lot. "She might. But no, she's glaring at me. It's nothing, really." I brush it off. "So you finally got enough money?"

"Yep. Well, technically, I had it a few days ago. My roommates got tired of seeing me mope, so they got together three hundred dollars between them to loan me. Though now I have to do everyone's dishes for three weeks."

"You could afford it last week? Why'd you wait so long to go get it, then?"

"Ah...well..." he says, tapping the steering wheel with his palms as we turn onto the strip, a long, straight road that runs parallel to the ocean and is packed with tourist attractions, including the Pavilion. Jude continues, "This is weird, but... until the other night, it was like I had musician's block. I couldn't write anything."

"What changed?"

Jude inhales, is silent for longer than he usually could stand. "I went back to the ocean."

Something in me stops, alarmed, unsure. "When? What happened?" Did you meet Naida? Lo? Did you remember she's really your Nightingale? Questions I'm afraid to ask...

"The other night, late. I didn't get in the water, but I stood on the shore. And I got an idea for a song."

I'm relieved, and ashamed of it. He should meet Naida. He should know she saved him. I should tell him.

"What's the song about?" I ask instead.

He pauses. "It's a love song. A sad one. I think it's about the ocean."

"About almost drowning?"

"Maybe," he says. "I'm really happy with it. I just haven't been inspired, and then the other day..." He shrugs. "I got over musician's block, I guess. Maybe it's the Nightingale syndrome inspiring the romantic in me." He says the last bit offhandedly, like it's nothing, but it makes me blush. When he looks at me, he laughs a little, but there's a nervousness to it that's as charming as it is awkward.

The music store is between a pet depot and the remains of a closed water park where the slides are cracked and awnings ripped, but the sign still promises the park's returning next summer. The music shop is empty, save the older man behind the counter, who recognizes Jude immediately. He leads us over to the wall covered in guitars—acoustic, electric, expensive, and ones so cheap that I wonder if they even play.

"How do you know which one to buy?" I ask as Jude runs his hand across them.

"You can just *feel* it."

"Really?"

"No. I researched it online and figured out I want this one," he says, tapping one in the center of the display, then grinning at me. I roll my eyes at him as the old man nods and vanishes to the stockroom to get the guitar.

"Play the song you were talking about to me," I suggest, but he shakes his head.

"It's just an idea right now. I'll need to work on it—oh, that's it," Jude says as the old man returns. Despite Jude's joke about "feeling" the right instrument, he turns the guitar over in his hands, holds it a thousand different ways before nodding and handing over three hundred dollars in wadded-up cash and a blue credit card. When we leave, he looks a little overwhelmed; I notice he keeps looking in the mirror to see the guitar in the seat behind us.

"Are you okay?"

"Yeah. It's just the last time I bought a guitar, I was fourteen and, stupid as this sounds, it changed my life. It made me feel like... *me*." He stops and looks at me. "I never really thought I was going to be a rock star or anything. I just wanted to create something beautiful."

"What did you want to be?" I ask.

"I just wanted to get out," he admits, pulling out of the parking lot. "What about you?"

"It'll depend on what Anne and Jane do."

"What do they want to do?"

"I don't know that they've thought about it, either." That's not entirely a lie—there are dozens of psychic reading places along the strip, promising tourists summer love and sunny vacation days. We've talked about opening our own one day, but it's mostly a joke. Yet at the same time, their powers are the only thing Anne and Jane love to do. What else could they possibly become?

"You know how you said you think you aren't like your mother yet?" Jude asks. I nod. He pauses, then speaks. "I think you will be when you embrace being Celia, instead of just being Anne and Jane's sister," he says. I glare at him, and he shrugs. "I know, I know. But maybe being *Celia* is for you what playing music was for me. Wishing you'd left me in the water now, aren't you?"

"At the moment, maybe."

"There were other people on the pier, you know." I stop glaring, raise an eyebrow at him. He slows at a red light and looks at me. "There were plenty of other people on the dock. You're the only one who ran down to save me."

"I was the only one who knew the way. If you aren't familiar with it, that road by the church—"

He looks down, a little sheepish. "You were the only one. And you didn't even know me. I was just some clumsy idiot, as far as you knew. I know Anne and Jane are your sisters, but I guess all I'm trying to say is that you're enough without them. Even though you seem to doubt that."

"It's not them," I say before I can stop myself, defend myself. "It's that I don't always like being me very much. Or at least, I didn't."

"Didn't? What changed?"

I pause. One moment changed everything, and in none of the ways I would have expected. I turn my head to look at the guitar in the backseat as I answer. "You fell."

CHAPTER SIXTEEN

Lo

"And then you twist this side over," I explain. A girl older than Molly but a few months younger than me sits beside me in the sand, in the area where the *Glasgow* split, watching as I wind my fingers through Key's hair. "And that keeps it from getting tangled." The girl nods, studies my hands carefully, then does the same on the girl sitting at her feet. It's a silly way to pass the time, but not without its merits, I guess—if you don't keep your hair braided at the height of storm season, it'll be a tangled mess.

"How did you learn?" the girl asks.

I smile a little. "When I first got here, another girl taught me. She's an angel now, though. You'll teach someone someday."

"Or I will," Key sighs. "I'll be here forever."

"Don't be silly," the young girl says. Her voice is *almost* bell-like, but there's a slow, twisted pattern to it, something that reminds me of Celia's voice—I guess it's her age, her humanity, coming through. "You'll grow old soon enough."

"Not nearly soon enough," Key jokes, but her voice is sad.

"Molly doesn't believe we become angels when we grow old," the young girl suddenly says. We all stop. I release Key's hair and the braid dissolves, flares up around her head. We look at the young girl, who quickly stares at her hands. "I don't think that's right, of course. But she's been telling people that lately. More and more."

"She's wrong," Key says sharply, voice almost a hiss. "And she's wrong to spread lies. What does she think happens when we grow old? We just...dissolve? Become sea foam?"

"She...she says she doesn't know. But that she just doesn't think we become angels," the girl says meekly.

"Well, I remember being on the beach. I remember the angel saying he would come back. Don't you, Lo?" Key says.

I nod. I remember it. It's just...now I know there's more to the story. There's a scream. There's a mystery....

But I don't say that. I can't say that to someone like Key. Either it would crush her or I'd lose her as my closest friend. I don't want to be alone.

Key sighs. "Come on, Lo," she says, extending a hand to me. "Let's go somewhere."

"Where?" I ask.

"Maybe to the edge?" The edge. The edge of the group, as far as we dare go—just beyond the rocks, where the *Glasgow* is almost out of sight.

"All right..." I say, and take Key's hand, confused. We leave the other two, letting the current do most of the work and push us away from the others. The current is tricky this deep—you think it isn't strong because you can't feel it tugging you, but you look up and next thing you know, you've drifted away.

"I have to ask you something," Key says, and her eyes are serious.

"Of course," I answer. We stare through the water. I should have tied off Key's hair, had her do mine. It's horrible trying to pick out the knots—I don't entirely blame the old ones for giving up altogether, letting their hair tangle like clumps of seaweed.

"Look," Key says, pointing through the water. I peer in the direction of her finger. Far away, there's a shadow moving, thick and slow. It carves through the water carefully, like it's moving each drop out of its way. A whale—behind it, a few more. There must be even more farther into the sea; they come in fifties, hundreds, sometimes. I grin, almost start toward it—

"What are you doing?" Key asks.

"I want to see them up close—"

"You can't leave us."

I stare at Key for a long time, then at my sisters behind her.

"What are you talking about?" I ask quietly, but the lie in my voice is screaming.

"Twice, at least. You thought we wouldn't notice?"

"Have the rest of us noticed? Or just you?" I answer.

Key looks down. "Just me." I can tell she hates it, that it isolates her to be the only one, which means she might—

"You can't tell them." I cringe, as does Key, when I say *them* out loud. "You can't tell us," I correct myself. "Please."

"It's not safe out there," she answers. "Please, Lo. You're not acting like Molly, are you? Doubting the angels? Because...I don't want to feel about you the way I feel about Molly. I...I almost hate her." She drops her voice low at the last part, so low I almost miss the word. "So please. What are you doing out there?" she asks. I back away from her slowly, letting the water cradle me as I lean into it. I look up through the ocean. I can barely, barely see the stars.

"I'm..." I stall for a long time.

"Tell me, Lo! I'm your sister. You always have to tell your sisters."

You're one of my sisters. I had another. A long time ago. I shake my head, sigh. How could I explain Celia? Walking up on shore to meet with a human girl who gives me back memories that I quickly forget again? It doesn't even make sense to me, to be honest. And Key would never understand—more than anyone else, she's always been happy to forget her past. Happy to embrace the ocean; in fact, it was her love for our sisters, for this life, that made me finally embrace it. She can't understand this. And so instead of the whole truth, I give Key a fraction of it.

"There's a human boy," I whisper. "I'm meeting with him."

"A what?" Key asks, her face sparking. "Where did you find him?"

"The boy I saved from Molly," I admit.

"Molly's human? Oh, she'll be furious!" Key says, and I wonder if she'd have the same delight if it was another girl's human.

"You can't tell Molly," I say swiftly, grabbing for Key's shoulders. "You can't tell any of us."

Key looks confused. We don't keep secrets. She rocks backward in the water for a moment, thinking about what I've said.

"Are you afraid someone will try to steal him?" she finally asks.

I shake my head no.

"Well, are you going to try it, then?" she says, sounding impatient.

She doesn't need to clarify what *it* means. She wants to know if I'm going to drown him. If I'll sing him into the water and pull him under and see if his soul can become mine.

"I...I'm not sure yet."

"You're waiting? That's wise, I suppose, since we all know he won't love you quickly. I still can't believe you're going to the surface like this. It's so dangerous, Lo. You're so brave. But if it worked...if you gave him time to fall for you..." She pauses for a long time. "I guess I'd have to be an angel without you."

I force a sad smile. "If you're an angel, you'll be so old you'll have mostly forgotten me, anyhow."

Key laughs a little. "That's true. None of us really leave

the ocean—we aren't ourselves when we become angels, after all. It's like we only live for a little while, isn't it? As humans, as sisters, but then in the air...angels live forever, don't they?"

"I suppose. I don't know."

"They do," Key says, voice confident. "So why would you want to be a human again, anyhow?"

"I just..." I search for words, how I can explain it to someone who has been looking forward to the air since we met. "I want to be an angel, Key. But I don't want to lose myself. I don't want to lose my human self, either."

"But...for things to be born, things must also die," Key says gently. "It's just the way it is."

I nod, smile at her. She's right. Julia had to die so she could become Key. Key will have to die so she can join the angels.

Jude would have to die for Naida to be reborn.

Of course, he'd have to love Lo first.

CHAPTER SEVENTEEN

❧

Celia

I take a deep breath. Just say it. "I think we should go somewhere."

Naida looks up at me from the steps of the church, where she's sitting. She's taken the shoes off; dried blood clings to her feet, but it's no longer flowing. The sun is nearly set in the trees behind us, and the scent of funnel cakes seems permanently attached to the breeze. I nod up toward the Pavilion, and Naida's eyes widen.

"What?" she asks, like she's genuinely convinced she misheard me.

"This beach, being here by the water. It's no wonder it's hard for you to remember, when everything that Lo loves is just a few yards away. We should try to go farther into shore."

"I can't. I can't walk."

"You can with the shoes on. Sort of. And I had an idea for that."

"I don't look like you."

"I had an idea for that, too," I say, and reach into my purse. I pull out a compact of powder makeup, one I stopped wearing because it's so heavy. I don't think it'll totally mask the blue of Naida's skin, but it'll help. Maybe at night, if no one is looking too closely, no one will notice she stands out. Besides, what would they say—"Excuse me, but your skin is blue"? No. They'll try not to stare and hurry their children along.

I think. I hope.

But this can't go on forever. Am I going to just keep coming here, reminding Naida of the life she once had? Caught between guilt over her actually saving Jude, hope that she'll remember, joy when my power helps? Naida needs to remember being human. And that means *being* human. No ocean, no sand, no endless watery horizon. We have to at least try. It's a weeknight; the Pavilion won't be crowded—even my sisters opted to go to the movies instead of coming down here. It'll be safe. It'll help—*I'll* help. It's my power. Maybe helping Naida is the thing I've been waiting for, the chance to be—as Jude said—*Celia* instead of Anne and Jane's sister. If that's the case, I have to be brave, bold. I have to be more like my mother.

Naida doesn't seem nearly as determined as me—she stares at her feet, licks her lips. I can tell she wants to go. She looks toward the Pavilion, closes her eyes. She nods.

I open the compact; Naida holds her arms out for me, and I smooth line after line of powder across them, swirling

143

it around her elbows, then across her back, everywhere the dress doesn't cover. Her skin is so smooth that the powder goes on easily, but it still looks strange against her skin, like it's Halloween makeup instead of skin-toned. Her face is trickier, since the darkest blues are near her hairline. We spend almost an hour trying to cover her, with me taking a few steps back, looking at the work, then running in to patch places.

"I think that's it," I say finally, nodding. Naida looks down at her arms, smoothes the dress, smiles.

"Do I look normal?" she asks.

No. She doesn't. She doesn't look human; she looks like she's in a disguise. But there's so much longing in her voice that all I can do is grin and nod and hope that no one will ask questions.

She slides the shoes back onto her feet and winces as she takes a few steps out of the church's doorway, into the sand. I rush to her side, link an arm underneath her shoulders to help her. The path will be the worst part—if we can just get to the top . . . I look over at the people on the edge of the pier. They'll be able to see us from the halfway point, where the pier lights begin to illuminate the grass.

"See the light, right there?" I ask, stopping as we begin the trek upward.

"Yes," Naida says breathlessly. The fear is gone, replaced by excitement, eagerness.

"At that point, you have to walk on your own. Until we get to the top. Then I'll go get something for you—"

"What? Alone?" Naida asks, eyes jumping to me.

"If someone sees me helping you up, they'll think you're hurt. They'll try to help, and if they get too close, they might see..." I motion toward the powder on her arms, clearly streaked and fake when I'm right next to her. "You have to make it on your own, and you have to make it look like it doesn't hurt. Can you do it?"

Naida inhales, looks at the top of the trail. It's only about twenty feet from where the light hits to the edge of the pier, but it's uphill, through sea grass and sand—it's tricky to navigate even for me.

"Yes. I want to remember. I have to," she says firmly, and I'm not sure if she's trying to convince me or herself.

We start up the pathway. It doesn't take long for blood to drip over the sides of her shoes into the sand. She doesn't wince, doesn't cry out, doesn't even close her eyes when I stumble and she's forced to balance herself for a beat. When we get to the light, I look over at her and carefully, slowly, let her go. I motion for her to go first—if she falls, I want to be able to catch her. Naida presses her lips together, takes a step, another. . . . She leans down to use tufts of sea grass to tug herself forward, which I know must be slicing across her hands, but she doesn't seem to notice. People are starting to glance over at the girls walking up the side of the pier. No one looks twice. Yes, this is working, this will work—

Naida stumbles forward on the last step when the sand shifts beneath her feet. She throws her arms out, an action that would probably steady her in the water but does nothing on land. She falls on her chest, scraping her face in the sand. Someone's walking over to help her; he looks concerned—

"She's fine," I say—snap, even—from behind Naida. I struggle to run the last few steps, kneel to help her up.

"Are you sure?" the older man says. His hair is speckled gray, eyes doubtful.

"Yeah. She's drunk, that's all," I say, giggling like it's hilarious.

The man rolls his eyes. "Damn kids," he mutters before walking back to the corn dog stand.

"Are you all right?" I whisper to Naida as I help her stand. The makeup on one side of her face rubbed off when she hit the sand. I whip the compact out and try to cover the blue again—though it's actually not as noticeable here. It's easy to pass it off as the glow from one of the neon lights or the flashing rides.

Naida doesn't answer; she grabs hold of the edge of the pier and leans against it, digging her nails into the wood.

"Stay here," I say. "Just a minute." She blinks, like she's dizzy, but nods. I dart away, not far, but enough to make me feel panicked, frenzied. The booth is just ahead—

"Hi," I say to the woman inside the illuminated hut. She's wearing a dirty shirt with the Pavilion's logo, and her stomach presses against the edge of the counter. She stares at me.

"I need a wheelchair," I say. "My grandmother is winded—thought she could make it, but—"

"On the side," she says, pushing a key on a wooden stick

toward me. She thumbs to her left; I peer around the building to see a small row of wheelchairs chained up beside two golf carts. I slink around, insert the key in the padlock, and wheel one out. The woman doesn't look up when I slide the key back toward her.

The chair is hard to open and has PAVILION PROPERTY scrawled across the back in Sharpie, but it'll work. I zip through the crowd, wheeling it in front of me, almost running over the same man who tried to help Naida earlier. When I reach her, she's barely moved, like she's afraid she'll fall much farther than a few feet if she releases the railing.

"Here," I say, setting the chair up behind her. I grab her shoulders and pull her down into the seat. She exhales, breathes heavily for a few minutes, then gives me a weak smile.

It isn't packed by summer standards, but still—there are so many people. I wish I could see Naida's face, or even that I had Jane's power and knew what she was thinking. She grips the arms of the chair tightly, her head turns side to side so fast it's like she's watching a tennis match. There are a few stares, but they're only in passing; we move mostly unnoticed through the masses. I pull the chair around several food carts, near the outskirts of the Pavilion. There's a calliope on this side, and a bench meant for sitting and watching it play music—though, just like I suspected, no one is here. I wheel the chair to the bench and sit down. Naida listens to the haunting organ melody for a moment, stares at the paintings of trees and woodland creatures on the sides, before turning to me. She's smiling, but she looks sick. Not just sick, but like she's been sick for a long time—the sort where the person looks wasted away, broken.

"This is amazing," she whispers. Her voice shakes. Light bounces off her cheeks, making the circles under her eyes look even darker.

"Most people don't appreciate it," I admit. "And I probably wouldn't have ever realized it was here, except for the fact that it backs up to the parking lot. See that spot in the fencing? You can push it in. My sisters and I sometimes sneak in here during the off-season, when it's all creepy and empty...." I drift off, grin at memories of us running through the park, free and boundless and happy. I look back over at Naida—she's gazing at the calliope. No, staring, staring like she can't force herself to look away—

"I remember...." she says shakily.

"What?" I ask when she's silent for a long time.

Her gaze finally drops to the giant carriage wheels that hold the calliope up. Her lips curl into a smile. "I remember my sister," she says breathlessly. "I remember how we used to fight, but I also remember how much I loved her. And I remember school, how I was terrible at it and how it made my father angry. And his face, I almost remember his face...." A few tears form in the corners of her eyes, escape, and slide down to her collarbone. "There was one of those traveling fairs that used to come to town. It set up in the Piggly Wiggly parking lot and had awful rides—I mean, they were all old and beaten up. But there was this calliope, this old calliope with brass pipes and carvings all around the edges. Every carving showed a different myth. You know, Psyche and Cupid, Odysseus and Penelope, that sort of thing. And every year when I was little, my dad would tell me the story behind one of the carvings, until I stopped thinking it was cool to go to the carnival with your dad and...there was one left. There was one he never got to tell me."

"Did you know what it was?" I ask lowly, like any volume to my voice would shatter the memories she's building.

"I looked it up," she says, nodding. "After he died, I think—I remember crying when I found the story. It was Philomela and Procne. A story about these sisters who get turned into birds. Hardly anyone knows it. I asked at the carnival why it made it to the calliope, but none of them knew. Their great-grandfather carved it, and they couldn't remember how he chose the myths." She smiles a little. "Maybe you could've found that out for them."

Naida sighs happily and slumps back in the chair, inhales deeply, like she's drinking the scent of a nearby popcorn machine. The calliope finishes its song, making the area seem quiet for a moment; the relative silence is quickly filled up with the noise of rolling Skee-Balls in the arcade and a child throwing a tantrum over a snow cone.

Naida sighs, turns to look at me. "Why do you think it chose me? Whatever made me Lo, whatever changed me... why me?"

"I don't know. Maybe there's no reason."

She looks away. "Maybe I was just unlucky."

"But we can try to change it," I say quickly. "Your luck, we can try to help you remember. Your future doesn't have to be like your past."

"How do you know?" she asks, turning to me, and I realize I have no answer because I don't know, and yet, I firmly believe it's true.

"Come on," I say instead, rising. I grip the back of the chair and push her toward the midway, near the front of the Pavilion. Her breathing is raspy, heavy, the way I think it would sound if I tried to breathe underwater, but she doesn't complain, so I keep going. There are rows and rows of booths with people trying to conquer silly tasks, like knocking over milk bottles or tossing balls into peach baskets. People are carrying around giant stuffed animals, balloons in the shape of swords, and wearing their new airbrushed beach T-shirts. Children have their faces painted with butterfly wings or tiger stripes, a few with images of dolphins leaping from their cheeks.

"Where do you want to go?" I ask, leaning forward so she can hear me.

"Anywhere," she says. "Everywhere."

So we keep walking. I want to take her into the café, but there's no way she'd pass for human under the stark fluorescent lights. And we can't exactly go on the rides...so we wander. Around and around till my arms hurt, but Naida doesn't seem to be bored or tired. She nods at sights, looks up at me, and grins weakly, each time looking a little sicker, a little more tired.

I should suggest we go back. I should tell her she doesn't look well.

But I don't want to. I want her to get better, I want her to stand up without pain, I want her to be human and never go back to the water.

I see the boys coming before she does.

They're a few years younger than me, probably drunk on summer freedom and the lack of nearby parents. They tumble through the crowd loudly, knocking people out of the way, oblivious to everything that's going on except the game they're playing. Water guns, the pump kind, that they must have won from a booth over by the waterslides—an area I very specifically didn't take Naida. I rise as they near, shooting carelessly, unaware of the chorus of anger around them from people who didn't want to get wet. A security guard is coming to stop them, but he's slow, he's too far away. They get closer. I step in front of Naida, just as one of them shoots his gun straight up into the air beside us. He bumps into Naida's chair, laughs an apology, then continues on—only for a few more feet, before the security guard reaches them and they disperse.

"Sorry," I say, brushing the water off my arms—at least it hit me and not her. "Come on, let's go look at the Ferris wheel." I turn to her.

"What?" she asks, and her voice is strange. She's holding

her fingers in front of her face, rubbing them together, staring at the place where her thumb and forefinger meet. I narrow my eyes and realize there's a single drop of water between them.

"Naida..." I say slowly. Her eyes look darker than before, the circles under them more pronounced. Sicker, by the second, even, like she's dying. She coughs; she can't breathe. Something rises in my chest, panic, worry—what have I done?

"Water," she says. "Take me back." Her voice is different, not Naida's voice. Lo's voice.

I grab the handles of the chair and push, walking fast, hurry, go, go, not so quick as to draw too much attention, but her skin is starting to show through the makeup, her breathing is louder, she's tilting forward in the chair like she's lunging toward the ocean. The pier is ahead; I can see the ocean. Naida—Lo—tilts her head back, inhales, like she's breathing in the water's nearness. I slide the wheelchair to a stop at the edge of the path. I don't care if anyone's looking; it doesn't matter. I move around, thinking I'll need to help her, but Lo springs from the chair and runs forward, down the path, and into the darkness. I hurry after her, but the change in light is too much. I can't see anything. I stumble and fall, slide through the sand and brush, down to the shore.

Sand in my eyes, my mouth. I cough, try to spit it out, clamber to my feet. The tide is in, the ocean is near... I take a few unsteady steps forward.

"Naida? Lo?"

No answer. My eyes finally adjust, and I kneel down at dark marks in the sand. Footprints, thick with blood that pools into the deeper area where her toes pressed into the sand, running desperately. I follow them toward the waves. One shoe, then the other, kicked off as she fled into the water. I step on the edge of one of her footprints, and the blood tints the tips of my toes.

She's gone.

CHAPTER EIGHTEEN

Lo

I'm sorry.

That's what I want to say. I know she was trying to help Naida. I know she cares about Naida.

But I'm not meant for the shore. I tear the dress off my body, turn in the water. I breathe deep, let water fill my lungs, course around me. My body aches, muscles sore and skin tender, like it's been burned. The shore was killing me. Naida was killing me, even if she didn't mean to.

I don't want to lose myself. I don't want to die. But neither does Naida.

CHAPTER NINETEEN

❦

Celia

Naida was supposed to meet me a few hours ago—seven o'clock, our usual appointment. She wasn't there. I waited by the church, but she didn't come.

Will I ever see her again? The way she left, the pain, the panic... That was Lo, though. Naida wouldn't just leave like that, vanish forever. Unless Lo is stronger now, able to keep Naida from emerging, from surfacing...

No, don't think like that. I swallow, try to break apart the tension in my chest. Just outside my bedroom door, Anne and Jane are checking each other's eye shadow. I have enough to worry about tonight, with the two of them. They're still angry with me over keeping Naida a secret; I can't let them see I'm worried about something, not when we're supposed to be having a real night out together for the first time in ages. A night I'm genuinely excited about, no less.

"Promise you won't read him?" I say seriously to Anne and Jane as we're about to walk out the door.

"Jesus, Celia, we can be normal human beings for one night," Jane says.

"Last time you guys saw him, you read him. It's not a crazy thing to expect," I argue.

"Fine, no reading Celia's boyfriend, Jane. I won't, either," Anne says. "Or at least, I'll try really hard not to." I glare at her, but she grins back. I sigh as we walk down the dormitory hallway, heels clacking on the tile floor.

"Shotgun," Jane calls gleefully when we burst through the dorm's front doors.

"I thought you were driving," Anne grumbles as we head to the car. I take the backseat.

We drive out of the main tourist section of the beach, down to a tucked-away area behind the canals. It's an antique-looking part of town, all salt-battered wood and faded paint, filled with old families and crab fishers. There's a coffeehouse here, one I've heard of but never been to. Apparently, after dark it becomes something of a coffeehouse-music-venue-bar where two of Jude's four roommates are playing tonight. Jude asked us to come—well, Jude asked me, specifically, but Anne and Jane wanted to go and he said that was fine—that his roommates could use the crowd and would probably be more than happy to occupy my sisters after the show.

"Look at the three of you," Jude says when we park and get out of the car. We're probably overdressed, but Anne

156

wouldn't have it any other way. Jude is smiling, though, so I suppose we don't look too ridiculous. "Anne, right?" he says, pointing to Jane.

"Wrong. Is anyone else coming?" Jane answers, looking around at the gravel lot occupied by only us, Jude, and a handful of crows picking over discarded hush puppies. The trees overhead are thick with wisteria vines and Spanish moss, leaving the dimly lit coffee shop looking spooky, an island of light in the darkness.

"Of course. There's a drunk who comes here every night for the cheap beer," Jude says. "Plus the waitresses."

Anne and Jane don't look miffed, though; rather, they look somehow delighted. Maybe it's just because it's different from the crowd they're usually engulfed in. They eagerly order lattes and take the best seats in the place, an oversize love seat with dusty upholstery. Jude's roommates are setting up on the plywood stage—they look like they belong in a box set with Jude. Same type of clothes, same messy hair…They call him up to help arrange some equipment. Anne and Jane look over at the table where I'm sitting, pushed up right against the arm of their love seat.

"Are the roommates off-limits for reading?" Anne whispers, giggling.

"They're not even your type!" I should frown, should be annoyed, but I can't draw up those emotions.

"Maybe we've been trying the wrong type," Jane answers. "I like the blond one with all the tattoos. What's his name?"

"I have no idea," I say.

157

"Hey! Blond guy! What's your name?" Anne shouts. The blond roommate looks up, gives Jude a quizzical look. Jude chuckles and shrugs.

"Um...Derron," he says.

"His name's Derron," Anne tells Jane, who dissolves into a fit of laughter.

As promised, a drunk guy *does* show up, but so do a large handful of other people, enough that when Derron and another roommate take the stage, there's a decent round of applause. I get my own latte and a chocolate croissant, which Jude pays for before I can stop him.

"So are you as good a musician as them?" I ask.

"Well, it's an unfair comparison. I mean, there're two of them," Jude points out, grinning. I roll my eyes at him just as they begin to play.

They *are* good. Not amazing, not revolutionary, but good. Derron is on piano, the other one on guitar, and they cycle through a series of songs about girls they once loved, places they once went, making metaphors I don't always understand. It's just loud enough that to be heard, Jude has to lean in close to me; he smells like soap and honey. I jump a little when he puts a hand on my back, drums his fingers along to the music, but the layer of fabric between us keeps his memories safe from me. The air feels sugary and thick, between the coffee steam and the music, and I forget to notice time passing, hours passing. When they finish, it's nearly one in the morning.

The drunk leaves, but most of the crowd stays to talk—I

realize just about everyone is friends with one or both of the musicians. Anne and Jane see this as a delightful challenge and thrust themselves to the front of the crowd. Despite his initial wariness, Derron seems to be charmed by Jane, and the other guy doesn't stand a chance at deflecting Anne. I feel a little guilty, but only a little—I can't control what my sisters do any more than they should be able to control what I do, really.

"Come outside. I want to show you something," Jude says lowly. I meet his eye, try to figure out what he means, but he isn't giving away his secrets. He rises; I follow, slipping out the coffee shop door so quietly the bell doesn't even jingle— not that Anne or Jane would have heard it above the roar of conversation and laughter going on by the stage.

It's quiet out here, muggy yet cool. Jude walks over to his car and pops the trunk, then stands in front of it.

"Don't make fun of me," he says seriously.

"What?"

"That song I was talking about at the music shop? I wrote it."

"Really?"

"No. I wrote the music, and the words for the chorus. But it's something."

"And you're going to play it for me?" I ask.

"I planned on it, if it doesn't make me look like one of those guys who sit on Milton's campus playing just to pick up girls."

"My sisters love those guys," I say, laughing a little.

"Of course they do," Jude says, shaking his head. He opens the trunk and pulls out his guitar, then shuts it and sits on the hood. He motions to himself. "See. Sitting. Not walking. My odds of falling into the ocean are greatly decreased." He waits for me to smile, then looks down at his hands for a moment.

"You play for people all the time," I remind him when I realize he's nervous.

"People. Plural. I've never played for just one person, actually. I'm trying to figure out where to look."

"Maybe at your hands? That way you can avoid awkward eye contact," I suggest. A grin flickers across his face.

"See? Always helping." Then he starts to play—looking at his hands.

He hums along in the places there are no words, but with confidence—he knows every note perfectly, and they're clear, unmuddied by the sound of his left hand sliding up and down the neck. And then he gets to the chorus. *The ocean doesn't mind, it doesn't care, / It's too refined for people swimming, people dying, people loving, people trying. / And in the shadow of a temple, where the ocean finds its prey, / That's where she's waiting for me, by the water, by the waves.*

It isn't until he's halfway through the chorus that I realize he isn't looking at his hands anymore. He's looking at me. It makes me feel warm, makes my fingers feel tingly, like they're about to fall asleep. Jude plays through the rest of the song, singing the chorus once more, quieter this time, like he's telling me a secret. When he finishes, he exhales, waits a few moments before pulling the guitar strap up and over his neck. He busies himself putting the guitar away while I try to find something to do with my hands.

"Do you want to know what I think?" I ask.

"Only if you promise to lie to me if you hated it," he says, closing the trunk and turning to face me. *Why didn't I wear something with pockets? Then I could put my hands in my pockets instead of standing here like an idiot....*

"I liked it," I answer. "Very much."

He hesitates, leans forward, speaks quietly. "Are you lying?"

"No. Really."

"Excellent to hear," Jude says. He steps toward me, sways a little. "Do you tell your sisters everything?"

"I used to," I admit. "I don't anymore."

"Let's say a really handsome guitarist were to try to kiss you. Would you tell them?" he says.

"It's possible."

"Would you slap, kick, or otherwise injure said guitarist for trying?"

"It's possible."

"Hm. Risky," he says, tapping a crooked finger against his lips. I can't stop myself from smiling, nor can I stop the nerves bubbling from my stomach to my head. I don't want to see his past. I want him to share it with me. I want to be normal. I want this to be normal.

161

He steps closer.

"Trivia: What's your middle name?" he asks, voice low.

"Ruth. Yours?" I'm whispering, though I don't mean to be.

"Thomas. Barnaby Thomas. My parents were really determined for me to get beat up in middle school," he says, voice hushed as he grows closer, closer.

I'm terrified.

Jude takes my hand—I feel the memories start. They jolt through my fingers. Flashes of childhood—falling off bicycles, catching lizards in a woodpile, being switched for coming home after dark. His hand runs up my arm, but I can't appreciate it. I want the memories to stop; I don't want to see Jude this way again. It isn't fair. He touches my collarbone, my cheek, and then before I know it, his lips are on mine.

And the memories stop.

The wall is up, built instantly, because I can't possibly read his past when I'm so, so busy with the present. He kisses me, and I step closer and kiss him back. He tastes like coffee and salt water and sweetness, and I lean into him. I feel brave, I feel reckless, I feel all the things I never thought I'd be able to feel because of the power.

When he pulls away, our hands find each other's easily.

"Don't look now," he whispers, letting his eyes leave mine, "but there's a small chance your sisters and my roommates are staring at us." I whip my head around to the coffee shop. The window is crowded with the four of them and a few random onlookers, laughing and making faces at us. Anne and Jane look both delighted and horrified at once. They're going to tease me mercilessly when we get home, I can tell.

But they're my sisters. It's their job. We're stronger together.

CHAPTER TWENTY

Naida

I'm able to push to the front of my mind as soon as I break the surface of the water—Lo falls back easily. I think she might be letting me win, though, letting me control the body we share to make up for her bolting from the Pavilion last night. Or . . . I think it was last night. I can't tell—I feel like I've been asleep. Celia is already on the shore, looking at me worriedly as I emerge from the waves. I smile at her.

"Are you all right?" Celia asks, handing over the shoes. I slide them onto my bleeding feet; ocean water and blood slicken them quickly. She's holding a piece of fabric—a dress, since I suppose the one I was wearing when Lo took over is lost to the ocean now. I pull it on quickly, grateful that Celia is averting her eyes.

"I'm fine. I'm sorry about . . . the Pavilion. It was Lo, she was just...she suddenly was so strong, too strong for me to stay...here." In my own body, *the body that was mine long before it was Lo's*, I think bitterly.

Celia pauses a long time. "I was scared when you didn't meet me the other day."

"What day is it?" I ask.

"Wednesday."

"Oh. I didn't even realize..." Five days? I lost five days? Celia seems to understand and nods. We walk toward the church together; she swoops in when pain shears through my feet, lets me lean on her. It's different now than it used to be—instead of constant pain, it's a dull ache punctuated by moments of absolute agony, like a knife is scraping away my bone.

"It's like Lo got sick, so I got sick," I explain. "When we were away from the water, I mean. The longer I was away, the worse it got, and the more desperate she got to go back."

"It was a stupid idea, anyway. I should never have convinced you—" Celia starts.

"What would we have done instead?" I ask. We reach the church. I lean away from her, sit on the church steps. "Sat here. Again. Talking."

"It's better than you being in pain," she says.

"Is it?" I ask. "What if even when I remember everything, I can't leave the shore?"

Celia is silent. She sits down next to me. "Then..." She draws half circles in the sand with her toe. "Then we'll have to renovate the church, because it'd be a god-awful apartment as is."

We laugh together, and it warms me, like the summer air is evaporating more than just the water from my skin.

"So," Celia says after a few minutes pass, "Jude and I...we sort of...we kissed," she confesses, biting her lip.

"Really?" I ask, not even trying to hide the gleam I feel in my eyes.

"Yes," Celia says. "It wasn't what I expected. But that was what made it good."

I wait, try to relax my mind, hoping that her story will finally trigger a memory I confess I long for—something romantic. Something about a boy who loved me, or a boy I loved, something sweet and perfect that will make me feel like a normal girl again. Nothing comes. I grimace, hold out my arm for Celia.

"Help," I say, sounding meek. "I can't find it on my own. Did I have a boyfriend? Did anyone want me like Jude wants you?"

"I...I might not be able to find it. That sort of thing is usually hidden—"

"Behind the screaming," I say, sighing.

"I'll try, though," Celia says hopefully, and touches my arm lightly. She waits a long time, longer than usual. I hold my breath. I hope I had a boyfriend like Jude—not like him, exactly, but...funny. Clever, the kind who tells jokes. I don't care if he was a musician, but maybe something artsy, like a painter or—

"I...I don't see anything," Celia says. She opens her eyes, meets mine. "I don't see anyone, or any memories of kissing."

"I've never been kissed?" My voice sounds small, not at all the way it usually does.

"Or it could just be a really deep memory," Celia says quickly.

"Yeah, maybe," I say, but I don't believe her. I've never been kissed, and now my skin is blue and I live underwater.

Maybe I should just leave now. Go back to my "sisters." They understand me; they're my home. Why am I playing at being human again? Remembering when you had a soul isn't the same as having one. And underwater, everything is beautiful, quiet, perfect....

"Naida?"

I inhale sharply, jerk up. Celia is looking at me, pity in her eyes. I stare back. Why is she helping me?

"Does he love you now?" I ask.

Celia's face falls a little. "Lo," she says quietly.

Lo? Am I Lo? No, I'm Naida....I'm Naida, but I'm buried, watching Lo speak through my lips.

"No," she finally answers my question, sighing, "or, I don't know. Love doesn't happen that fast."

"I know. I tried to make a boy love me once."

"What happened?" she asks, voice frigid.

"He drowned. I drowned him. I had to try it. It's the only way we can get a soul. Make a human love us, then kill him to take his."

Celia jumps a little, leans away from me a little, studies

167

my face. She's afraid, she looks sick. She's right to be. She takes a breath, reaches forward—her hands are shaking, and I feel bad. I didn't mean to scare her any more than I meant to drown the boy. Celia places her fingertips on my shoulder delicately; I flinch at the feeling of her skin on mine—everything feels so dry.

"Your sister's name, it started with a C. No, an S." Her voice is thick, like she's keeping herself from vomiting.

"*Sophia.* Her name was Sophia. Oh, I remember." I crumple forward, put my face in my hands. It feels like everything in my chest is falling, bursting into flames, pushing Lo aside until I control myself again. *My sister's name was Sophia, and she was three years older than me. I remember. I remember her.* Tears drip through my fingertips and onto my lap. Celia sighs and wraps her arm around my shoulders, her skin hot compared with mine.

"How could I forget my sister's name?" I cry. Celia strokes my hair back but doesn't answer. "I keep getting lost," I say, finally looking up. I inhale deeply, try to fight the feeling of collapse in my lungs. "I forget, and then I get stuck being...being Lo. Even though I am Lo, I know I'm her. But I'm also Naida."

"I know," Celia says. "I know. Don't stop trying to remember, though."

I look at her, shake my head. "It's so hard to be both. It's hard to be either, but I can't be both forever. It's like..." I inhale, searching for a comparison, and only one comes to mind. "It's like Lo is killing Naida. I can feel it. Again and

168

again. I go into the water, and she kills me. Buries me, holds me down. I want it to stop. I just want to be myself again, all the time, not...this."

We sit in silence for a minute. My dress is hiked up and the straps are slipping off my shoulders, but I don't care. My feet ache, my heart aches, everything hurts and tears at me. The ocean will fix all that. It'll make the pain stop. It'll heal my wounds. It'll kill the memories that gnaw at my mind, at my heart. I watch the waves lapping at the shore, look beyond them to the deep water. How do I live out there? I lived in a house, a house that was also a store, with my sister and a dog. That's where I'm supposed to be. It isn't fair that I'm here; it isn't fair that I somehow became...this.

Nothing is fair.

"Celia?" I say.

"Hm?"

"Don't trust Lo." I turn to look at her; she's silhouetted in the setting sun.

"I don't," she says firmly. "I can't. She's a murderer, she's...I'm afraid of her. But I trust you."

I face the water, nod. "Good. Lo is confused; she's desperate. You can't trust someone that desperate."

CHAPTER TWENTY-ONE

❧

Celia

In the days following Naida's warning about Lo, I dream about one of two things: Naida or Jude.

The dreams with Naida always end the same. I tell her all the memories I see in her head—her sister, her house, her room, even her favorite book, but every time I tell her about a memory, she gets lighter and lighter, until she's faded into nothing but white light. And then that fades, too.

When they're about Jude, they're...

Well. They're different. They involve kissing, of course, they involve breaths and whispers. But moreover, they involve touching. His fingers on my collarbone, my arm, my waist, skin-on-skin and yet no memories, no screaming in my head. Nothing but the simple perfection that is him touching me. And then I'll wake up and be amazed to realize that the touch isn't just a dream anymore, that it's real. I can stop the memories now. I can hold them back and just feel...everything.

But tonight my dreams aren't sweet—they're of Naida. In the dream, she's fading fast, fast, her skin is getting bluer, she looks more and more like Lo as I frantically call out things to remind her of who she is. I plead with Lo to let Naida go, but then they vanish into the waves, and I'm alone on the beach, in the church—which, in the dreams, always looks more like some sort of temple to the ocean, with the mermaid girl from Jude's tattoos painted on the walls. I call for her, run to the water, drop to my knees, but she's gone. I failed. I couldn't save her. My power is as useless as I always knew it was—

I sit up in bed, startled by the darkness compared with Naida's white light in the dream. It takes me a moment to figure out where I am, for my heart to stop racing. I blink, try to figure out what woke me.

"Shh. It's just me," Jane says. "I was just shutting your door. You're talking in your sleep." I jump at the sound of her voice, then look toward the doorway at her silhouette.

"I left my door open?" I ask groggily, surprised.

"Yeah. Don't worry about it. Go back to sleep."

I nod, lie back down as she clicks the door shut. *Go back to sleep.*

I'm not sure I want to.

CHAPTER TWENTY-TWO

Lo

"You're here again," I say, surprised. I almost didn't put on the dress—I didn't the last few nights, when I came here and sat on the beach alone. Tonight, though, I wanted to see if I could hold on to myself even in Naida's clothes—especially since I notice her voice is growing ever louder in my mind each time I surface. It's lucky I put on the dress, I suppose... though for a moment, I wonder how he would react if he saw me without it.

"Yeah, well, I wanted to say thanks, and this is the only place I know to find you," Jude says. I press myself against the church wall, into the shadows—the moon is bright tonight, and I'm afraid he'll see me. "The thing you said about the ocean. It was sort of the kindling for a song I wrote."

"*You* wrote the song. You don't need to thank me for that," I tell him.

"Maybe..." Jude says. He puts his hands in his pockets, sways a little. "But I feel like you put it in my head. Like a muse. Is that weird?"

"Yes."

"Oh."

We're quiet for a few moments, listening to the waves.

"How did you know I'd be here?" I ask him, keeping my eyes trained on the water.

"I didn't." Jude shrugs. "I just thought I'd check. Are you all right?"

"You asked me that last time."

"Last time it was because you were crying. This time it's because you look...sick. Green, sort of."

"I'm fine."

"Really?"

"Yes," I say, looking away. How long can I continue tricking him into thinking I'm human if he's already noticing it? A cloud passes in front of the moon, and I almost sigh audibly in relief. If he knew what I really was, would he run? He should. If he's smart, he'd run and never look back.

Jude sits down in the sand near me, just out of arms' reach. "So, what are you really doing here all the time?"

I could give him another short answer, an answer that doesn't really answer him at all. But I'm tired, and I'm starting to wonder if my sadness makes me more human than even Naida's memories do. I look his way, hoping he doesn't notice how dark my eyes are. "I'm trying to remember the girl I used to be."

"Used to be?"

"A long time ago. She was happy; I'm not."

Jude nods knowingly—really *knowingly*—before speaking. "I'm familiar with being miserable with your life. I understand."

I don't know how to answer, so I stay quiet.

"I played the song for a girl," Jude finally says when the silence is too much to bear.

That's right, he played it for Celia—I remember talking to her about it, but only vaguely. Those memories belong to Naida. "She loved it," I say, perhaps a little too knowingly.

"Yes. It seemed a little weird, playing a song for one girl that was inspired by another."

"I inspired the song, or just the parts about the ocean?" I ask, raising an eyebrow.

Jude looks sheepish, guilty. "Both. I'm not sure why. When I look at you, I think about music. It's like you're singing to me even though you aren't."

I nod, look down. Molly sang to him, sang our songs to him. He thought they were beautiful, but not for the right reasons. Not for the same reasons he thinks Celia is beautiful, not for the same reasons he might love her.

"Play it for me?" I ask. He looks up.

"I'd have to go get the guitar from my car," he says, but he's already rising to do so. I nod, and he turns to hurry up the path, like he's worried I might vanish before he gets back. I sigh as the clouds move away from the moon—it's risen so that moonbeams are streaking down straight onto the side of the church. I can't stay here, not without Jude realizing that my skin color is far too wrong for me to simply be sick.

I rise, let a cry of pain escape my lips, but I force my feet along the beach, toward a section shaded by the shadow of the pier. The sand here is a little wetter since it's closer to the water—it still hurts, but it's not quite as excruciating to stand. Being closer to the waves also makes me calmer, like it slows down my heart, soothes my mind the way the water soothes my wounds.

Jude jogs back down the path, guitar over one shoulder. I see a moment of panic when he realizes I'm not by the church, but then he finds me.

"You moved," he calls out.

"I do that," I answer through teeth gritted from the pain. I have to relax—he'll know. I keep waiting for him to come closer, but he's frozen up by the dry sand, staring at something. I follow his line of sight out to the waves.

"You're still afraid?" I ask.

"I liked what you said about the ocean," he answers, "but that doesn't change the fact that I almost died. I can't stop thinking about the way it felt underwater." He looks between me and the waves, like he's afraid to take his eyes off either of us. He can't move.

I can. It hurts, but I can. I force myself to stand straight, to walk forward—still in the shadow of the pier but closer to the dry sand. The urge to cry out is overwhelming, the urge to drop to my knees and crawl even more so. But I can't let him see, I can't let him see. The shadow hides the trail of bloody footsteps behind me as I grow closer, closer. *Please, stop hurting me*, I beg as it burns through my stomach, around my shoulders, behind my eyes.

"Thanks," Jude says when I'm nearer to him. I nod, sink to the ground. I want to cry. I don't. Why didn't I just go into the water, disappear?

Because I want to hear his song. Jude turns the guitar around to his front and positions it. He looks at me, then starts to play, keeping his eyes on mine. I feel trapped, locked in his gaze, but I don't dislike it. I don't dislike it at all.

The song sounds like the ocean—it rises and falls, notes splash forward and harmonize with the sea behind me. It sounds like one of our songs, I realize. The one Molly sang to Jude the night I saved him. I close my eyes; the song makes me think of home. It makes me forget the pain, the hurt, the longing. It makes me feel like I did underwater before all this happened, before Jude, before Celia—it makes me feel peaceful. No conflict, no doubt, just me and my sisters and the ocean all around us.

I open my eyes and begin to sing.

My words and Jude's music turn around each other in the air, matching the ocean, matching the darkness. Jude is still looking straight at me, his eyes widening as each line leaves my lips. We've long forgotten where our songs came from, yet we never forget the lyrics even when we're old. Jude takes a step toward me, another; his face is still, his eyes locked on mine like he's seeing something beautiful for the first time. Another step. I continue to the next verse.

Yes. Come to me.

Another step. I back up. Closer to the waves, closer to the water. *Follow my song, so I can pull you under*—the voice in my head feels dark, like it's not my own.

I shiver. No, no. I don't want to drown him. He says he thinks of music when he looks at me. He turned our song into his own—he must feel something. . . . Could he love me? Is it possible?

I'm afraid the answer is no. But he's drawing closer, mesmerized, following me as I back up toward the water . . . and I find I'm equally afraid the answer is yes.

It would be easy. Naida would be human again. I wouldn't forget myself and become an angel. I'd be a real girl, like Celia. I could run on the beach and be seen by others and go find my family—

No. I am Lo, and I don't want to kill him. But I can't stop the song; it feels like it's forcing itself out of my mouth, like it isn't really *me* singing. We take another step toward the water. Part of me wants to drown him so, so badly—I want to dive into the water, let it encircle us both. Pull him to the bottom and kiss him in my home, in my world. I want his soul. How can I just walk away if there's even a chance I could have it . . . ?

No.

I force my lips shut.

Jude continues playing for a moment, then wakes up— the smallest of the ocean waves lap around his feet. He stiffens, then clambers backward into the sand.

"How . . . ? I was just—" he begins, looking confused. He shakes his head, rubs his temples, glares at the water like it tricked him. He doesn't look at me. He doesn't suspect me. I walk forward, out of the tiny waves. My toes curl up from the pain.

"Sorry," he says. "I don't know what happened. That was weird." He looks up at me. "You have a beautiful voice."

"Thank you," I say. There are tears in my eyes, but I hold them back. Jude shakes off the last of my spell, turns the guitar over his shoulder. He takes another step away from the water just for good measure. It's a little while before he speaks again.

"Who are you, really?" he asks me.

I stare. "I'm no one. Just a girl on the beach."

"You're different, though. I told you, I look at you and I think of music—"

"Maybe you should stop looking at me, then," I say. A tear falls, but I look away before he sees it. When I turn back, Jude is looking at the ground.

"I can't stop looking," he mutters. "Besides, it's like I told Celia. Once you get involved—"

"Celia." I say her name like she's a stranger. "You should go to her. See music in her."

"I . . ." he begins, but he doesn't know how to finish the sentence. Finally, he starts a new one. "Can I help you, Lo?"

"With what?"

"With whatever makes you come to the beach in the middle of the night, alone."

I look down, shake my head. "No. It'd kill you to help me."

"No, it wouldn't," he starts to insist, stepping forward, hand outstretched. I step back.

"It would," I whisper. I turn to look down the shoreline. "I have to go."

"I can drive you—"

"I'll walk," I answer, and before he can say anything else, I start toward the darkest part of the beach, knives carving into my feet each time they hit the sand.

CHAPTER TWENTY-THREE

&

Celia

Students will be moving back into the dorms again in a few weeks. Our little island of solitude on the outskirts of campus will become packed with parents and students and boyfriends and bags from bedding stores. I see all the signs: a few teachers moving in early, the fire alarm they keep testing, the reminders to register for classes. Anne and Jane are currently on a quest to be excused from science this year, hoping they can pass the senior exam and prove they already know the material. It helps, of course, that right before the test, Jane plans to brush against the proctor and see the answers. We get a check from our uncle to purchase a new set of uniforms—khaki skirts and blue shirts, which every girl at school will inevitably hike up or down, whichever makes them look more scandalous. Still, none of this seems real, like school and Jude and Naida and my sisters can't all possibly exist in the same universe.

We spend Saturday cleaning our apartment—sort of. Mostly, the three of us are watching a stream of terrible crime shows while halfheartedly throwing things from the main room into our own bedrooms, then shutting the door quickly, like the clutter might escape.

"I remember this episode," Jane says, when the third hour of a crime show starts. "The brother did it."

"Why bother watching it, then, if you know what's going to happen?" Anne asks.

"By that logic, why do you bother *living*?" Jane answers, giggling. Anne and I laugh. I feel like what happened at the coffeehouse with Jude started to heal something between us, some wound that existed long before I met Naida. Maybe because kissing Jude means I'm more like them than they thought. More like them than *I* thought.

"We should go to a movie tonight," Anne suggests after a series of trailers plays on the screen. The movie theater at the end of the strip is pretty impressive, since there's not much else to do on a rainy day at the beach. We haven't been in ages.

I nod. "We should. But you're not tricking Jude into paying for our tickets," I say, only partially joking.

Anne throws a pillow at me. "We won't! But maybe... you could invite that girl. The one who knows about your power."

The room falls silent, save a peanut butter jingle on the television.

"You said eventually," Anne adds. "Eventually we'd meet her. She knows about your power. We deserve to know her."

"It's not like that," I say quietly. "She can't...she can't come out."

"What are you keeping her a secret for?" Jane asks, and I suddenly realize that my sisters have been preparing this conversation for a while now. They're well rehearsed, like they're reading lines in a play.

"Because, she's just...It's complicated."

"No, it's not. She's your friend. Why can't we meet her?" Jane says.

"Look, she's not going to tell anyone about my power. I'm using it to help her. She wouldn't ruin that. She's just a girl—"

"If she were just a girl, you'd have introduced us. We're stronger together, Celia. We always have been. I don't understand why you're letting someone change that," Anne says.

"I'm not changing that!" I argue. "I just want to be strong on my own, too. I want to be able to use my power for something good. I want to be able to talk to someone, to have friends outside of you two—"

"You have Jude!" Jane says.

"Why doesn't *he* bother you?" I ask suddenly. My sisters don't answer. Anne rolls her eyes at me and yanks open a cabinet door, begins piling plates inside like she's punishing them.

"I'm serious," I say. "Jude and Naida are both new friends; you don't know either of them that well. Why doesn't he bother you?"

"Because you aren't lying to us about him," Anne snaps. "He's here. We've met him. We can read him."

My eyes narrow. "You said you wouldn't."

"And we won't," Anne says. "But we could. And we could know if he was bad news, and we could help. I mean, if he turns out to really just have Nightingale syndrome or some other weirdo girl-who-saved-me fetish, we'll know about it." My face heats up with anger. She continues quickly, holding up her hands. "I know, I know, maybe he just likes you, maybe it has nothing to do with saving him. My point is, we're supposed to help one another. We're not supposed to just...go meet mysterious people from the water and pretend that's normal."

"I never said she was from the water."

"What?" Anne says, like I'm talking crazy.

"I never said she was from the water. I never even mentioned the water." I can hear the anger in my voice. I feel hollow. They didn't. They wouldn't.

Anne and Jane look at each other, briefly, a flicker of movement. But it's enough to know that they did.

I feel my blood speed up in my veins.

"You read me?" I say, voice high and shrill. "Not as a joke, not to be funny. You were trying to find out—"

"Relax," Jane says. "I only went after the things about Naida. I didn't just look at everything in your head while you were asleep—"

"That's supposed to make me feel better?" I snarl. I feel tears in my eyes, but I won't let them fall, not now. I'm shaking—everything is shaking. I've never been this angry, this...I force myself to breathe; the air gets caught at the tension in my throat.

"You were lying to us!" Anne says. She's not sorry—not at all. She slams the cabinet shut and stares me down. "You wouldn't tell us anything about her, and she knew about our powers."

"*My* power!"

"Ours!" Anne answers. "They're ours. All of them. You're not in this alone, Celia, and it's selfish to pretend like you are. I needed to know at least who Naida is, and it turns out, we don't even know *what* she is."

"She's just a girl!"

"She's a lot of things," Jane says. "But she's *not* a girl. You know that."

"She needs my help, that's all!"

"Then why didn't you tell us the truth about her? You think we'd care, that there're more freaks like us in the world?" Anne says.

"Because she wanted to be kept a secret," I say, folding my arms. "And unlike Jane, I respect people's secrets."

"Did she say that?" Anne asks. "To not tell us?"

"Of course!"

"No," Jane says, voice hard. "No, she didn't. I saw your mind. You were never thinking about keeping her a secret for her sake. You were always thinking about keeping her a secret for your own sake. Not I *can't* tell my sisters—I *don't want* to tell my sisters."

I inhale, try to argue, but the words hang. Is she right? Yes. Yes, she's right. Naida never asked to be kept a secret. Lo didn't even ask to be kept a secret.

"I wanted to have something," I say, throwing up my hands. I'm not sorry, I refuse to be sorry. My mother wouldn't have been sorry.

"Something without us," Anne says sharply.

I look up at her, drop my voice low and dangerous. "Exactly. I wanted something without you. Something the two of you weren't in control of. And you couldn't handle that." Jane looks like she's about to speak, but I cut her off. "So you read my thoughts. You knew what it would mean. You went prying through my head like I was just another stupid boy you've brought home—"

"*We had to!*" Anne shouts.

"Lies!" I yell back. "We're not stronger together. We're just...stuck together because we're afraid to be apart. I'm not afraid anymore, and you two can't stand it."

"We're all you have—" Jane starts.

"Right now, I'd rather have nothing," I snap, and before they can say anything else, I grab our car keys and storm out the door.

CHAPTER TWENTY-FOUR

Lo

Molly is sitting alone.

She's talked too much of her doubts about the angels. She's never said what she believes happens to us when we grow old, but her doubts are heresy enough among my sisters. While most of my sisters are on the *Glasgow*'s deck, Molly is out near the rocks that wrecked the ship. She has her back against one, and with her left hand, she draws shapes in the algae that covers them. I watch her for a moment pityingly, but I can't stay long—I want to go to the surface tonight. More specifically, I want to see Jude tonight. I swim around the back side of the *Glasgow*, where it'll be easier to get away unnoticed. Does he think about seeing me during the day? I wonder...

"You're going to the surface," a voice says sharply. My head snaps up—Molly. She came around the other side of the ship. Her eyes are sharp and bright; her words aren't a question.

"What?" I say, trying to sound confused.

"Key was trying to make me feel better about losing the boy, trying to convince me he would only have loved you anyway. I asked how she knew that, and she told me everything. Going to the surface, meeting with him . . ."

I curse Key silently. I should never have told her. "It's nothing," I say, but my voice betrays me, cracking at the lie.

"You stole him from me," Molly hisses. "Fine. He's yours. But I want one, too."

"You want . . . one?"

"Another boy. If you're strong enough to go to the surface and meet with one, so am I."

"It's not like that," I say. "It's not . . ."

"Not like what? I'm younger than you, Lo. If *you* still care, you know I must. We're the only ones left here who give a damn, who want to go back—"

"I don't want to go back," I say suddenly. "I mean, I do. But . . ."

"But what?"

"That's not why I'm seeing him. I lied to Key." I inhale, pause. "I'm not going to take his soul. I just . . ."

Molly's eyes widen, but not with anything resembling understanding—it's more like horror. "You love him?"

"No, that's stupid."

"Then you won't mind if I make him love me," she says, turning her head to the side.

"No!" I almost shout. "No, I don't know if I love him. I don't . . . I just like seeing him. I like talking to him.

187

But Molly, I don't want to go back. I'm not Naida anymore—"

"Naida. You remember your name."

"I remember *her* name. She's not me. Not anymore. I'm Lo."

"Lo isn't real," Molly says, voice dangerous. "She's just a shell. It isn't fair for you to do this, to go to the surface, to have a boy right there for the taking and not help me."

"It's never fair—"

"It could be!" Molly shouts, shrieks almost. I'm sure it woke some of my sisters. I look up at the *Glasgow*'s railing nervously.

"He wouldn't love you, anyway, Molly!" I answer, patience snapping. "You remember being human so well, you remember your name, but you don't remember how love works? You can't just make them fall for you, and even with time, they might love someone else. They might love another girl...." I drift off, realize there's a thickness in the back of my throat that accompanies a mental picture of Celia. Celia and Jude, kissing, holding hands, walking on the shore without pain or blood...

"You're right about that. I remember *everything*," Molly whispers, hate lacing her voice. "I remember more than you. You have a boy on the shore, you have a *chance* to go back, and yet I'm the one who remembers what really happened the day we changed. I'm the only one who can still remember, so I'm all alone. I'm stuck down here like I'm being punished when all I did was watch my sister get torn to shreds and—"

188

her voice grows louder until the moment she stops short, and I realize she's crying, sobbing, even, though the rage in her eyes is still clear.

"You remember what happened?" I say softly. I look up to see one of my sisters peering over the railing; I smile and wave her off. There will be more, though. They'll all be curious. I have to talk fast—

"Of course," she says. "I don't know how the rest of you could forget."

The screaming in my head—Molly knows. As hard as I have to fight Naida at times, I still have to know what happened to her. "Tell me, Molly."

"Ha," Molly says darkly. "You won't help me. Why should I help you?"

"Because then you won't be alone."

Molly studies me for a moment, hair floating in the current—she's stopped braiding hers, and it's messy and tangled. "Do you remember your sister?"

"Yes," I say. "A little. She was older—"

"No. Your *twin* sister."

I pause. "I don't remember a twin." Even as I say it, though, I remember something Celia said once—"It feels like there are two, but I never see the other's face, never see any sign of her." Maybe that's who she saw—a twin? But what does it matter—

Molly flinches at me, like I horrify her. "You had one. She was just like you. She was just like you, and she was killed. It could have been you, it could have been me, they didn't care.

It's just one had to die so the other could come here." She speaks fast, angrily, bitterly, and it becomes clear her words aren't really meant for me. They aren't really meant for anyone. "They murdered her. They tore her to pieces like a doll. They didn't listen when I begged and screamed—"

"Who?" I finally interrupt. Molly looks up at me like I've startled her.

"Your angels," she hisses, then turns and swims away.

CHAPTER TWENTY-FIVE

&

Celia

I stay away from my sisters as much as possible. Come in late, leave early. I don't want to talk to them. I don't want to see them. Is this what it felt like for my mother, when she left her family behind to marry my dad? Becoming more like her isn't quite what I expected.

They aren't even sorry. They still see it as something that had to be done. As much as I've come to appreciate my power over the past few weeks, I can't help but wish it was something more along the lines of shooting lightning from my fingertips. I know exactly who I'd strike.

I spend most of my time at Jude's place, even when he's away at work. The apartment he shares with his roommates is a dive. A clean dive, but a dive. The furniture is beaten, none of the plates or cups match, and bills with PAST DUE are categorized on the table—a pile for things that are serious when they say PAST DUE and a pile from companies that won't be serious for another few months, according to Jude.

None of that bothers me—and it doesn't seem to bother Jude, either, really. We sit on a blanket-covered couch, windows open and box fans blasting, watching DVDs of eighties cartoons. They're funny and stupid and clever, entertaining enough that between the shows and a box of banana Popsicles we're able to forget the blazing heat. And I'm able to sometimes forget, at least temporarily, that my sisters betrayed my trust. That I don't know how to help Naida. That I don't know how to banish Lo. How is it that I'm here with Jude, growing happier, while Naida can't even leave the shore?

"You look worried," Jude says. It startles me; I jump, then shrug.

"I'm fine. I'm just...I don't know. I'm mad at my sisters, but I hate being mad at them. And I have this friend Naida who I'm sort of worried about. I just..."

Jude nods, drums his fingers against my shoulder—it's getting easier and easier to stop his memories from filtering through to my mind, a fact that makes me smile despite everything. "Why are you staying mad at them, then? Why are you worrying about your friend?"

I look down. "Because I'm tired of them expecting me to be nothing but their sister. I feel like what I want is more important than me just smiling and nodding. And I worry about my friend because I'm the only one who can help her, so I need to. I want to."

"Ah. Anne and Jane's sister no more," Jude says, a little teasingly, and kisses my palm. "What *did* the three of you fight over, anyhow?"

"I...I don't want to talk about it," I say with a sigh. This doesn't seem like the time to bust out an explanation of how we have powers.

"Would it help if I made you lunch?"

I raise an eyebrow. "Made me lunch? Are we in a fifties sitcom?"

"No, but I'm an excellent cook. I make peanut butter sandwiches better than any of those television chefs."

"So by 'cook,' you mean...peanut butter sandwiches?" I ask, grinning. Jude lifts a hand to my chin and kisses me quickly.

"It involves more than one ingredient. It counts as cooking," he says, and rises from the couch. "If we just ate more Popsicles for lunch, see, that wouldn't count."

Jude walks to the kitchen and pulls down paper towels to put bread on. I get up, lean on the counter across from him.

"Can I ask you a question?" I say hesitantly. He nods. "You don't...I mean, the Nightingale syndrome thing. That's not why you're here. With me. Right?" Anne's suggestion that he really does only want me because I saved him, like some sort of pathetic pity romance, it got me more than I want to admit. But I don't want to hear theories from Anne or Jane—I want to hear the truth from Jude. *And whatever he says, I'll believe*, I think steadfastly.

193

Jude puts down the peanut butter–laden knife and looks up at me, concerned. "You don't really need me to answer that, do you?"

I inhale. "I . . . yes. Yes, I do. I just need to make sure."

He looks a little hurt but nods. "It has nothing to do with you saving me, and it has everything to do with you saving me." I don't say anything. Jude licks his lips nervously, comes around to my side of the counter, and leans beside me. "No one, in my entire life, has ever done anything for me. I mean, sure, my mom bought me school supplies, but then she forgot when the first day of school was, so I was two weeks late. No one has ever risked anything for me or . . ." He shakes his head. "But you went after me in the ocean, in the middle of the night. And you didn't even know me. So . . . yes. That's why I'm here. Not because you saved me, but because you're the kind of person who saved me."

"What if I hadn't?" I say warily. Because I didn't save him. Not alone, anyway.

"Then . . . I would be at the bottom of the ocean?" he jokes. When I don't laugh, he answers seriously. "You'd still be the kind of person who *would*. But that aside, Celia, you're interesting. You're fun to talk to. You're beautiful. And you don't fall asleep when I talk about guitars, which is more impressive than you might think."

I smile—*Has anyone ever called me beautiful?*—then open my mouth. I should tell him, tell him about Naida, about Lo, about how I didn't save him, I just watched as she did. About how I tried to do CPR, but I was afraid of all his memories hitting me at once. About how I lied to the EMTs, the doctors, to *him*.

But I can't. I would have saved him. I would have, if Lo hadn't. Right? And that's what matters. That's what he cares about.

I feel guilty when he leans in, drops his hands down, and interlaces his fingers with mine gently. But when his lips meet mine, the guilt melts away. I build the wall in my head, stop his memories before they flood my mind. Everything is deliciously normal. Perfect. Beautiful. For the time being.

CHAPTER TWENTY-SIX

It's the middle of the day, when most of us are sleeping, splayed around the *Glasgow* like decorations instead of girls. I am awake. I feel like I'm always awake lately, thinking about Molly's words—*your angels.* She hasn't spoken to me since, but I haven't stopped thinking about what she said. The screaming, her twin sister...Did I really have a twin? Did she die so I could become this? I stretch back along a group of rocks into an area where the tiniest amount of sun penetrates the water—so small that I think I may just be imagining it. I close my eyes, try to relax despite the thousands of thoughts and questions running through my mind.

A shadow passes over the light ahead. I ignore it at first—it could be any number of things. Dolphins, fish, sharks... but then I feel something brush the skin of my waist. Finger-tips, hair, maybe, and my eyes spring open.

I almost cry out in surprise but manage to keep the noise hidden. Above me, directly above me, breaking apart the tiny trace of light I found, is one of the old ones.

She looks dead.

She blinks. No, she's alive, of course she's alive—she's just old. She drifts with the current; it sways her limbs and her hair around her body. It's terrifying and beautiful at once—she looks like some sort of flower, something caught in the water. Everything about her is perfect. Smooth skin, dark eyes, lovely hair.

She is frighteningly beautiful. I feel like I'm hypnotized just looking at her.

And she is leaving. She moves up, up away from me slowly, then faster as the upper current takes hold. I watch, entranced, until she fades from sight, off to become an angel.

Your angels.

I snap out of it—this is my chance. I look around at the rest of us; we're all asleep. I can follow her if I go now. I can ask the angel why Naida was changed. I can ask him if there's a way to keep me and Naida alive, if there's a way out of both of us dying. I can find out if he and his kind really did murder Molly's sister, if I had a twin. I can ask him a million questions that no one else can answer.

I'm terrified, both because of what Molly said and because knowing the truth might be much harder than believing the fantasy.

Yet I push down on the rocks and jettison upward. The old one isn't swimming, isn't struggling; she's merely being carried along. I'm afraid to get too close to her, and afraid of the surface at midday, so I follow along deeper in the water. I wonder if Key would have come with me. I wonder if Molly would have come.

An hour passes, then another. I keep waiting to see something spectacular—wings blooming out of the girl's blue-toned back, sunlight streaming through her body and lifting her out of the ocean. Nothing. We're getting close to the shore, not the shore with the church, but someplace farther south. What if someone sees her? Plucks her from the water, thinking she's a drowned human? What if they see me? For a moment I wonder if I should grab her arm, pull her deeper, where it's safer, but no...no, I want to see what would happen if I weren't here.

Even through the water, the sun directly overhead hurts me. I feel like it's drying my skin up. When I see the old one has broken the surface and is now facedown in the waves, I worry about the smooth skin on her back. Is it cracking? Is she in pain?

Where is the angel?

My sister begins to thrash. Fight the waves, fight the water. She can't swim, she can't breathe—the waves rolling into shore are starting to carry us, push us toward the sand. I panic, rush toward her, but a wave takes her body and sweeps her out of my reach. Don't worry, I'm coming, don't worry, we're in the shallows now—

The old one slams her feet into the ocean floor. She rights herself, lifts her head out of the water, and gasps for air. I pause, watch as she takes a step, then another, then another, away from the sea, out of the water. She can't walk on the beach—what if people are nearby? The angel has to be here somewhere; he'll protect her....I peer through the water for signs of legs to indicate humans are on the beach. I see none—maybe this area isn't popular, maybe no one will see her....

I close my eyes and lift out of the water slowly, very slowly. Water breaks away from the crown of my head, and I can feel the sun searing my scalp. The midday sun is nothing like the gentle evening one I see when I'm with Celia. I rise until just my eyes are out of the water, leave them closed for a moment while water runs down my forehead and lashes. When I open them, they tear up from the brightness.

Find her, find her—there. Just ahead, wading through the knee-high surf awkwardly, clumsily. Her skin is even more beautiful in the light; she looks like she's carved from smooth pale blue stone, but it's like she's forgotten how to move in the water.

Movement catches my eyes—an angel? No, just a fisherman. He's standing slightly down the beach, watching the old one with his mouth hanging open. He kneels and drops his rod by the bucket at his feet, grabs a battered towel, and takes a tentative step toward her. He's old and fat, with a round belly and a large, floppy hat on his head. I look back to the old one. No wings, no light, nothing. As she clears the smallest of the waves, I look down to her feet, expecting to see blood.

There is none.

The fisherman calls out to her—what will she say? What will he do? The fisherman approaches her, looking both enchanted and afraid. He holds out the towel for her, keeping it at arm's length.

The old one gingerly takes the towel from his hands, observes it. She carefully wraps it around her body, tucking it in at the top to stay put. The fisherman points back to his belongings; he's talking, but I can't hear him over the waves. He turns his back on her—

And that's all it takes.

She's on him instantly. Her arms wrap around his neck, her hair whips behind her.

I can't hear him speaking, but I'm certain I'll never forget the sound of his neck breaking. It shoots across the water, rattles my core.

I scream. I can't stop myself. The water absorbs the sound, mutes me, but I scream anyway, then tremble as I watch the old one release the man's lifeless body. She steps away delicately, like it was nothing. And then she runs. Up the beach, over shrubs, and around palmettos like a wild thing. She isn't a human, she isn't an ocean girl. She isn't an angel.

I see movement at the top of the hill she's running up. I recognize him even from this distance—not his features, exactly, but the way he holds himself. The way he watches the old one as she runs toward him. The way he looks at the ocean, the thick scars on his chest.

He's the angel, the one who brought me here.

There are others behind him, men, tall and handsome like he is. Other girls with blue-green skin like mine. The old one joins them to little fanfare, like they were expecting her, not at all horrified by what they've just seen her do. They turn and walk away, moving like one creature, like a pack, animals prowling.

A scream ripples through my head, a memory; I blink, feel Naida's voice bouncing in my brain. I remember, all at once, like I'm drowning in the memory.

Molly was right. He isn't—*they* aren't—angels.

They're what made me Lo.

CHAPTER TWENTY-SEVEN

Naida

My sister screamed. The monster was coming toward us. It had teeth; it was a man, yet it wasn't— a man's face, a wolf's teeth, a devil's eyes. We'd seen the monster before, the night it killed our father, the night its fangs slid through his skin like his flesh was tissue paper. We thought we'd fought it off. We thought we were safe, that our dad had made the ultimate sacrifice to save us.

Yet here it was again. Back. For me.

The house was in shambles, and the sweet scent of dinner cooking fought against the iron-laced odor of blood. A tiny sound escaped from my quaking throat as I pressed against the wall behind the display cases. Keep breathing.

The noise brought the monster's acid-colored eyes to mine. Old blood caked its greasy chin. It licked its lips.

"No!" someone screamed. My sister. She dashed across

the room, slid over the counter, and crashed into me, holding her arms out. If I were brave, if I were bold, if I were more like her, I would have pushed her away from me right then. But instead, I shook, buried my face in her long dark hair, and prayed. Make it all stop. Please.

The monster raced across the floor—it's coming, it's coming, closer. There were thick scars on its chest, perfectly straight lines the size of my hands, like axe marks. I stared at them uselessly while my sister pressed against me, like her body was strong, like the monster's claws couldn't rip through her as effortlessly as they had my father six months before. She shook her head, pleading, begging, furious, emotions slamming into one another.

She was raging, while I slowly became calm.

It's not that I wanted to die. I just didn't see the point of fighting anymore. It was easier to give in than to continue running from the inevitable.

I wrapped my arms around her waist and hugged her. She thought it was because I was so scared.

But it was me saying good-bye.

I stopped listening to my sister's shouts, ignored the thudding sounds as she threw anything within reach at the monster—a demon, a man, an animal, it was everything, everything terrible. It was darkness.

It took slow, deliberate steps toward us, claws clicking on the hardwood. I could already feel its sticky breath on me, the scent of rot on its tongue. I braced myself and, with *all the strength I had left, shoved my sister aside. She screamed.*

She screamed, and screamed, and screamed.

The monster lunged, and almost instantly, I felt his warm, smooth teeth slide into my heart. Not to kill me, no— to change me, to make me more like him. I remember the woods, and then things blur, things soften, time slows....I'm at the beach. The monster—he's not a monster now, though; he's a man, a handsome man—is showing me the ocean. Telling me about the other girls in the waves, girls who would help me until he returned for me.

And so I went into the water. I didn't understand anything, I didn't feel anything; my memories were already fading. I let them fade. I let myself forget. The present didn't make much sense, but it made more sense than the fragments of past floating in my mind.

I became an ocean girl.

I understand now: the reason we forget, the reason only the ocean can make us feel. The reason we need one another, and the reason that the old ones stop needing anything. It's because being one of the ocean girls is what happens when we're clinging to the very last, tiniest shreds of our souls. It's merely a stop on the way to becoming a monster. Not dead, not a human, not an angel. A monster, just like the thing that brought me here, hurt me, made my sister scream, and turned me into this. How did I ever think he was an angel?

Because I didn't understand. Nothing made sense anymore when I was there on the beach with him. I wanted to believe he was an angel—we all wanted to believe he was an angel—and so he became one, simply because he's all we remembered. Because he was the one who brought us together, who made the pain in our feet and minds and hearts stop. I touch the spot on my chest that used to be scarred.

Is there any going back?

CHAPTER TWENTY-EIGHT

❧

Celia

I go to the beach Wednesday at seven o'clock. The Pavilion is starting to look nearly abandoned, with just a few older couples wandering from slow ride to slow ride. They'll start packing up some of the street vendors before hurricane season gets here, and then eventually, the rides will come down in pieces to be packed away in storage for next year. I make my way down the path to the beach to see Naida waiting for me by the church door.

"Hi," I call out—she's so focused on the waves that I'm worried I'll startle her. She turns to look at me as I draw closer. It's not till I'm a few yards away that I realize something is wrong. She's not Naida; she's Lo, and the expression on her face frightens me. No, not her face—her entire body. Everything about her is slow, careful.

"I remember," Lo says. Her voice is quiet, even.

"What?" I ask.

She looks up at me. Water still clings to her skin, and she hasn't put on the dress yet. She looks like a Roman statue, a goddess. "I remember what the scream was."

My eyes widen. I wait for her to explain.

"We thought it was Naida screaming the entire time," she says. "But then yesterday I saw something horrible. I screamed. And I—well, Naida—remembered. It wasn't her screaming."

"Who was it, then?" I ask, breathless.

"It was my sister, Sophia. She was screaming at it to leave me."

I feel cold, stiff. Screaming like that for her sister, screaming like it was *her* being hurt, being ripped apart...

"It?" I whisper. Lo looks at me, then lowers her eyes, extends her hand. I take it gingerly.

The memory explodes through me, as if it were shot from a gun. The house, the twilight, the scent of rot mingling with something sweet cooking on the stove.

I cry out but hold on; Lo tightens her grip on my hand. The man, the monster—his chest is covered in scars, thick and heavy, and as I'm looking at them through Naida's eyes, his face breaks down. Nose shoots out, jaw cracks and lengthens. He becomes a monster, claws and teeth like a wolf, hands like a man. He runs at me, Sophia screams screams screams—

I let go. Inhale, slowly. I'm shaking. Lo waits to speak, waits until I've found my breath.

207

"No wonder you blocked it," I finally gasp, and let my head rest against the church.

"Yes." Lo stares out at the ocean for a long time before speaking. "I saw one of my sisters come out of the water. She killed a man. She broke his neck. It was easy for her. That's what made me remember."

I swallow hard. Lo turns to me.

"She walked away and joined others like her. Girls who used to live in the ocean, other men who are part wolf. And the man—the monster—who changed me. I recognized him."

"Did they hurt her?" I whisper. "When she joined them?"

Lo shakes her head. "They welcomed her. She's one of them now. A demon. Darkness. I don't know. But that's what I'll become. All this time, we thought we became angels when we grew old." She pauses, looks down. "Naida's sister—*my* sister loved me. She fought for me. *I* fought for me. But it wasn't enough. Why wasn't it enough?"

"I don't know. But Naida," I begin slowly, hoping the name will cast Lo away, "we can still change this. You'll remember, and you'll be Naida again, for good."

"How do you know?"

"Because..." I pause, try to look like I'm choosing from a plethora of reasons instead of searching for one. "Because we're going to make it happen. You're not dark; you're not a bad person. You're just a girl with something terrible in your past. You didn't have a choice."

Lo turns to look at me, something ghostly in her eyes. "I still don't have choices, Celia. Either I become darkness because I've grown old or I become a human because of Naida. *I die either way.*"

"But you're *really* Naida," I argue. "Deep down. I see your past, everyone's past, and I know it can't be changed. I can't take back what happened to you. No one can take back their past, but you can choose something different. We can figure something out. Don't give up." I hear the desperation in my voice. It clashes with the look on Lo's face.

"I'm really Lo, Celia. I'm just as real as Naida. I love my sisters and the ocean, I saved Jude, I wanted to remember my past as Naida. I'm not giving up. I just can't let myself become a monster. I can't let myself hurt people the way Naida was hurt."

"I…" She's right. Lo is real. But I can't give up on Naida. I reach out, touch the back of Lo's palm. "Let me help, please. There was a big swing in your backyard. Your grandmother read you stories there when you were little, and when you were older, you and your sister pretended it was a pirate ship and swung back and forth on imaginary waves so hard, one of the chains broke."

Lo looks out over the water. She exhales, smiles.

When she looks back at me, she's Naida again.

CHAPTER TWENTY-NINE

Naida

"Do you see a twin?" I ask, after we've sat for a while. It's Lo's question, really, but it's floating around our shared mind.

Celia frowns, touches my arm. "It always feels like there was another sister," she admits. "But I don't see her. Maybe she died when you were really young? Why?"

"There's a girl out there," I say, motioning to the water, "who says something to do with a twin is why I went from myself to Lo. Why they chose me, why the angel wanted me. She wouldn't tell me how or why, though."

"Just because you're a twin?" she asks, and I nod. Celia pauses for a long time, and when she speaks, she sounds queasy. "What about triplets?"

I turn to her, shake my head. "I don't know." I try to disguise the hurt in my voice, that Celia so obviously is horrified at the thought of becoming like me, but it doesn't work. She gives me a sympathetic smile and looks away, but I can tell she's still worried, still has questions. We both do, but I feel more and more like they'll never be answered.

I ask her to go before the sun is completely gone. She hugs me but leaves, glancing back before she takes the trail up to the pier.

I don't want to send her away. But I want to exist without her. I need to know I can exist without her.

My name is Naida Kelly. My sister's name is Sophia. We had a golden dog and lived in a house in the forest. One day, something dark came for me. My sister fought hard, but it won.

And now it's coming for me again.

I remember the house we lived in. Our father made things, sweets, like candied apples and chocolate-covered lemon slices. Deer grazed in the backyard, and my sister and I often fought like sisters do. I don't remember all of it, but that doesn't stop me from missing it. I wish I knew what my father's face looked like, what my mother's hands looked like. I wish I knew where my sister is now—if she's still alive, or if the darkness killed her after it took me. If she's still out there, I wish I could tell her that I'm going to be okay.

But I'm not. It's not going to be okay, because soon I'll be gone. Celia has faith, but she's wrong. I don't have a soul, I can't live on the shore, I can't erase Lo from me entirely, and Lo can't erase the darkness she's going to become.

I will miss Celia.

I'll miss my memories.

I lie down on my stomach, push my fingers through the sand. My sister fought for me, might have died trying. She was brave. She had to know she couldn't win. But she tried. She gave it everything; she was willing to die if she needed to. She went down screaming and fighting, a sound that's forever locked in my head, a sound I don't want to ever emerge from my own throat. The monster's teeth on my heart changed everything. But there is a way to change everything back. There has to be. There will be.

My name is Naida Kelly. My sister's name is Sophia. We had a golden dog and lived in a house in the forest.

And I'm not going out screaming.

But I'm also not going out without a fight.

CHAPTER THIRTY

❧

Celia

The idea of doing this makes me angry. Makes me sick, even.

I need Anne, and only Anne. She's the only one who can help me. But I know if I do this, she'll think I've forgiven her. She'll think that I've agreed that we're stronger together, that it's okay that they read me secretly in the night, creeping into my room like thieves.

It's not.

But I want answers, I want to help Naida, I want to be brave, and so I need Anne.

"I have to ask you something," I say to her a few mornings later, before I leave for Jude's. Jane hasn't woken up yet—I figure I'll be able to handle my anger at my sisters better if it's only one of them. Anne is watching TV, and the annoying weather thing keeps scrolling across the bottom of the show, muting the audio to alert us of an incoming hurricane. They're rarely bad here, but they're still something the weathermen like to panic over. It takes Anne a moment to look up at me—a moment I think she draws out to irritate me.

I can't believe I'm saying this. I can't believe I'm doing this.

"So you're talking to me again, now that you want something?" she says, voice cool.

"I need you to tell me my future."

Anne looks at me for a long time, then turns back to the TV, shaking her head. "Your future with Jude?" There's maturity in her voice, wisdom that surprises me—the mocking, even the anger, is gone. I'm not used to it, and it makes my stomach coil.

"No."

Anne raises an eyebrow, thinks for a moment. "With Naida, then."

"Yes."

She crooks an arm around the couch, watches me.

"And why should I do that, when last time we read you, you stormed out of the house?"

"Because I'm your sister. And I asked. And you do it all the time to total strangers, and I've never asked you before."

"That's the point," Anne says, shaking her head. "To total strangers."

I stare at her blankly.

"My god, Celia," she says. "You really are selfish."

"What are you talking about?" I snap, abandoning the fact that I need her help.

"I always thought your power meant you wouldn't be, because you understood where people came from. But..." Anne presses her tongue to her teeth, drums her fingers like she's trying not to yell.

"The powers don't work for me like they do for you and Jane. I've told you that. They aren't a game, they aren't cute, because what I find out when I touch someone can't be changed. The choices are already made, and sometimes they were horrible, and I have to know that. I have to feel it. So now I'm *selfish* because I won't use them like some sort of game?"

Anne's eyes widen. "You think our powers are a game?"

"You treat them like a game, and you can, because yours are easier to bear than mine."

"Celia..." She looks disgusted, furious. "You know what *can't* be changed. I have to know everything that can be. I see someone doing something terrible in their future, something horrible. I see suffering, and I want so badly to warn them that they just need to make a different choice, a new decision, and it'll all be different.... And sometimes I do, even, but it hardly ever helps. I can't untangle their lives to tell them what to avoid. I don't even know when it's coming...."

"And so instead you make them buy you ice cream?" I snap. I don't believe her game of "my power is worse than yours," not for a minute.

"Yes!" she says. "Because if I don't do something stupid

215

with it, then I won't do anything at all. I'll just sit here and let it eat me alive. I do something stupid with it because I want to learn how to block the power, whenever I want, so I don't have to be scared every time I hug you that I'll find out you die or get hurt or leave...." She slams her hands down on the coffee table, looks away, and blinks back tears furiously. Anne doesn't cry.

I look down, try to swallow the heavy guilt on my tongue but fail. Anger is still bright and flickering in my chest, but I don't know what to say, what to do....

"Forget it. Come on, then. Let's do this," Anne says, sniffling. She tosses down the remote and motions for me to sit near her.

"Wait, no. You don't have to...."

"You need to know?" she says, voice hard. I nod. "Then I'll do it." She pauses a moment, and her voice softens. "I'll do it. Hurry, before I change my mind."

I take the cushion beside her. She holds out her palms, waits for me....

"I'm afraid of Naida sometimes," I say. I don't know why I'm confessing this—it has nothing to do with Anne looking into my future. Maybe I just want to admit it to someone, to offer a confession in exchange for all Anne has just told me.

"Why?" Anne asks.

"When she remembers, she's...she's my friend. She's the only friend I've ever had, other than you and Jane. She makes me want to help her, she makes me feel...*powerful*."

"And when she doesn't remember?"

"She's Lo—she has a different name when she doesn't remember. She's a different person. I don't think she'd hurt me. But I don't know."

"Is that why you want to know the future? To find out if she hurts you?"

"No. I just need to know if she'll end up remembering for good or not. If I could just get her to hold on to her memories, she could be Naida all the time...." I shake my head. "It's not her fault she's like this. It isn't fair."

"It doesn't really matter if it's fair or not," Anne says. "This is her life now. She has to choose what to do with it. It isn't fair that our mom died, or that our dad has no idea who we are, or that our brothers get to spend his inheritance while we're stuck in school. No one has it fair."

"But Naida doesn't really have much of a choice," I say.

"Trust me," Anne says. "With a person's future, there's *always* a choice. Even if it doesn't seem like it." She glances around at our dorm room—our home. This isn't how teenage girls are supposed to live. We should have our exciting, beautiful mother. Our father, all his memories intact. Our house in the woods of Georgia, a regular school, summer jobs at the bookstore in Ellison. We shouldn't be alone here during the summer. And yet here we are. This is our life. She looks back at me. "The only time you don't get a choice is if you're stuck watching the past. Sometimes you have to look away." She pauses, smiles a little sadly. "Sometimes looking away means tricking a boy into taking you out for fondue."

I want to laugh a little, but it doesn't work, so instead I nod,

217

then push my hands toward Anne. She takes them, rubs her fingers back and forth over the skin on the back of my palm.

She doesn't speak; she raises an eyebrow.

I watch, waiting, blocking the memories that are trying to get from Anne to me—we're like a river flowing two ways, currents crossing. I sigh, release the wall. A sea of memories comes at me—I'm in nearly all of them. I watch us moving into the dorms for the first time, our brother Samuel helping move in our couch. Our father standing there, saying goodbye, even though he had no idea who we were. The Pavilion, Anne's first kiss, myself through Anne's eyes—her not-quite-matched sister who she desperately wants to fix, to make happy, to make fit in seamlessly with her and Jane—

Anne pulls her hands away.

"Well?" I ask, trying to shake off the less-than-flattering image of myself.

Anne's face is a little pale. She looks at a loss for words, like her tongue is too heavy to articulate what she needs to say.

"Anne, you're scaring me," I whisper.

"I can't tell you how it ends, exactly," she finally says. She puts her head in her hands, winds her fingers into her hair, and pulls.

"Why not?"

"Because there's nothing there. There's no future between you and the girl—the water girl. Naida. Whatever she is."

"We stop being friends—"

"You're not listening," Anne snaps, and there's so much

worry in her voice that I feel cold. "There's nothing there, Celia. There's no future because there's no 'you and her.' It's blank."

"What does that mean?"

Anne sighs, shakes her head. "What have you gotten yourself into?" she mutters before looking me in the eye. "It means," she says, voice serious, "either she dies or you do."

CHAPTER THIRTY-ONE

I used to look at my sisters and feel joy. Feel beauty, feel like we were all connected.

Now I look at them and picture them on the shore, snapping necks, running off with the darkness that made us this way.

They're so certain we become angels. If I try to warn them, try to tell them the truth, they'll ignore me, all but exile me. I'll spend the last of my time with them alone, like Molly. I want to cry, but it feels so pointless, stupid, almost, so instead I settle in the sand, tilt my head back, let the ocean rock me. Sometimes it's easy to think it really does love me.

If it did, could I stay Lo, stay the shade of gray between Naida's light and the old one's dark?

If I let Naida win, it means Jude will have to die—*if* he loves me. I don't know that it's true, anyhow, but he's the closest thing either way. He's the only one there'd be any point trying on.

If I stay Lo, I'll wind up like the others. Like the man who changed me. Dark. I wonder if it hurts, or if we can go dark as easily as the sky does. It didn't look painful for the old one. And a storm is coming, a big one—a hurricane. I'd change fast; it'd be over before I knew it. It's certainly the easiest choice.

But it isn't really a choice.

I can't let Jude die, not even for Naida. And if Lo is going to die either way, then I know what I have to do. Tomorrow, when the sun is at its height, I'll go to shore, and I'll walk. As far away from the water as possible, no matter the pain, no matter how much my body longs to dive back into the ocean. If it worked at the Pavilion that night, it'll work even faster in the heat of the day. I'll fall and dry like any sea thing stuck on land.

I'll die. But that's the only choice I have left—how it'll happen. I'm not letting someone else—something else—make that final choice for me.

I let my eyes drift over the *Glasgow*. Only a few of my sisters are in sight; most are still asleep, but they'll be up soon. Maybe I should wake them up, tell them. Tell Key, at least—I grimly think about her wistful looks at the surface, about her longing to be an angel. She wouldn't believe me. She may trust me, but my words aren't stronger than her dreams. None of them would believe me, really—or they simply wouldn't care enough to kill themselves rather than become monsters. I suppose that's fair—I wouldn't have started caring if I hadn't remembered Naida. Maybe you have to know your past to look to your future, to make a decision about it. And my sisters have no pasts; they only have the present, this moment, each fleeting second—

Except Molly.

I lift my head, look for her. She's not here; I wager she's back in the *Glasgow*'s back bedroom again. She would care. She's the only one who would care, the only one who would believe me about the "angels"—after all, she remembers how we changed. She knows the man who brought us here wasn't an angel. She must know we don't become creatures of the light when we're old. She deserves to know what *does* happen.

I rise, swim silently into the *Glasgow*. I have trouble remembering the way at first; I look in several open doors, find nothing but decaying furniture, the remains of dishes shattered on the ground. Finally I spot the ancient chandelier and go toward it—yes, Molly is here. I approach the doorway to the back bedroom slowly, prepared for her to surprise me again. She doesn't. In fact, when I enter the room, it takes me a moment to find her at all....

But there she is. Shoulders pressed against the wall, legs swinging off the top of a bookcase with ornate molding. I suppose the clumps of brown on the shelf are what used to be books. She looks down at me, and it seems to take her a moment to remember that she hates me.

"Lo?" she asks.

"Molly," I say, and she inhales, closes her eyes.

"*Molly*. Yes," she says. Her shoulders slump a little with relief. She drops down the front of the bookshelf to float in front of me.

"Did you forget?"

She doesn't answer me, and I know what she's doing—repeating the name to herself over and over and over, just like I did when I first remembered Naida.

"You can give yourself a new name, if you forget that one," I say.

"It's not the—"

"I know it's not the same," I say, trying to sound gentle when really, I want to shout at her—*I know it's not the same. I know better than anyone else here that it's not the same.* "Do you still remember how we changed?"

Molly stares at me for a long time, then parts her lips. "Most of it, yes."

"I do, too, now. The monster, biting our hearts, bringing us here—" I stop when Molly cries out a little, like hearing the memories articulated stings her mind.

"You don't need to explain. I remember," she says. "I remember that better than I remember my own name."

"I saw them," I say. "The angels. The monsters. The things that changed us."

Molly lifts her head, looks at me incredulously. "Where?"

"On the shore. They really do come back for us. That part is true. It's just now I know you were right—they aren't angels. We don't become angels." I explain to her what I saw quickly—the old one emerging from the water, joining them. Molly's face goes from shocked to angry—determined, even.

"That's not fair. I don't want to be like them. I don't want to be like this, but I don't want to be like them, either. Not after what they did to my sister. My sister, my *twin*..." She balls her hands into fists. "I can't even remember her name anymore."

"That's something I still don't understand," I say. "I don't remember a twin, and they didn't kill my older sister. Why did they kill yours?"

Molly shakes her head, like I'm irritating her. "You had a twin at one point. We all did. It has to be twins—he told me after he killed mine. Twins have one soul split up over two bodies. That's why when they kill one, the other body can be changed; it's already becoming soulless. So the monsters followed my sister and me, chased us, they caught her first, killed her, and then they changed me. They killed her so they could have me." She touches a hand to her chest, where I can see the smallest, faintest remains of a scar.

"What about triplets?" I ask, Celia's question flashing through my mind. Of course she doesn't want to be like me—and if she's at risk, I have to tell her.

"What about them?" Molly asks, confused.

"I have a friend," I say, swallowing. "The boy I'm meeting on shore—it's not just a boy. There's a girl, too. She's a triplet."

Molly laughs coldly, like I'm a child, stupid for meddling on the shore. "Then tell your friend to be careful of angels.

I'm sure they'd love to find triplets. Kill one, get two new ocean girls? What a prize."

I look down, don't know what to say. "Look, you're the only one I thought would want to know about them coming back for us, making us like them," I finally say. "I don't want to be like them, either. I'm going to the surface tomorrow. I'm going to walk until I'm too far away from the ocean and I…"

"Die," Molly finishes when I can't.

I nod weakly. "If you want to…come with me…" It sounds so stupid to say it aloud, but there it is.

Molly gives me a strange look, and we're quiet for a long time. Finally, she exhales. "Leave me alone." It's not a demand; it's a request. A plea. Molly sinks down in the spot between the old nightstand and the bed as I back out of the room, turn, and swim to the open center of the ship. I pass most of my sisters, swim to the deck, and find Key asleep by the cherub railing. They will be dark one day, and I can't help them. I can't convince them. I can't stop them, any more than my older sister could stop the monster from taking me. I lie down next to Key silently, but in my head I'm shouting, shouting loud enough for all of my sisters to hear.

I'm sorry. I'm sorry. I'm sorry.

CHAPTER THIRTY-TWO

Celia

I'm sitting with Jude on one of the wooden benches that face the Pavilion in the early afternoon sun. It's the last week of the real summer season, so the crowd is small but rowdy. They leap onto rides like warriors overtaking enemies, down cotton candy and Cokes like they won't eat for the next few years—they mutter about cutting their vacations short because of the oncoming hurricane, are dedicated to a goal of riding each ride before the park shuts down early in preparation for the evening's storm. Jude has his guitar, and has played a few songs, collected a few dollars in the case, but now he's mostly just making jokes at the tourists' expense. I'm trying to laugh, but it isn't working.

"Tell me what's wrong," he finally says. His eyes are serious, despite the fact that the noise from the strong-man machine is almost louder than his voice.

I don't know how to tell him without telling him

everything. All the things I've kept from him, the reason we met, what really happened when I pulled him out of the water. My power, even. Instead, all I've done is lie.

He hates lies.

I want us to be a normal couple. More than that, I don't want to admit I lied. I don't want to admit that if he has Nightingale syndrome, it's for Naida, not me. Jude pushes the guitar to one side, wraps his forearms and hands around mine.

I inhale. "Remember how I told you about my friend Naida? She…" When I pause, Jude laces his fingers with mine, runs his thumb along the side of my hand. I lean into him even though it's hot and we're both sticky with sweat.

"Something's wrong. Something serious," I finally say.

"What is it?"

How do you explain that the dark half of a girl who lives underwater seems to be dominating the human part of her personality? I sigh. More lies.

"She's different. And she remembers how things used to be a long time ago, and it's depressing her that she can't go back to that time. Does that make sense?"

"A little. What are you going to do?"

"I don't know. I don't know how to help her."

I rest my head on his shoulder, inhaling the scent of fabric softener and sunscreen as he thinks. "Maybe you can't," he finally says.

"I have to."

"But maybe you can't," he says. "I tried to help my mom

227

for years, and finally I had to realize that there was nothing more I could do. I tried, I did my best, but . . . I had to let go of the past, of our past together, and think about the future."

"It's hard for me to let go of the past," I mutter. "It's like a phobia."

Jude smiles a little. "I still can't let go of that fear of the water. I thought you and I might walk on the pier tonight, but I keep avoiding the subject because the prospect of it makes me dizzy." He smiles at me a little.

"Come on," I say, rising. I offer him my hand.

"I shouldn't have said anything," he says, glumly taking it.

"Probably not," I agree. We start toward the pier. Rides are beginning to shut down, lines of angry people sent away. The hurricane isn't supposed to be big, but they always take warnings seriously.

The pier juts out ahead—with the dark clouds, it looks like it's a bridge straight into the storm. I remember seeing Jude playing here the night we met, before everything changed. One stupid board sticking out from the pier changed everything.

I feel Jude's hand tense as we grow close. It'd be easier if I looked at his memories, saw what he's remembering about the night—then maybe I could help him through those areas.

But instead, I ask, "What are you thinking about?"

"About how right here, I was playing a song I wrote about an ex-girlfriend. Maybe me tripping was her revenge." He tries to laugh, but it's a choked sound. He pauses as we step from the pavement onto the pier's wooden steps. "It was the worst feeling, drowning. I remember when I felt your hand on my arm, pulling me up. I thought you were an angel."

"An angel?"

"I know it sounds stupid, but yeah. How else could anyone have found me in the middle of the water, dark like it was, if she wasn't an angel?"

Naida. She's his angel. I'm just pretending. How long can I keep this up without telling him the truth?

We walk down the center of the pier, far from the railings. Jude is meticulous about where he puts his feet, walking slowly, carefully. We get to the spot with a new floor plank that replaced the one he fell over, yellow compared with the dingy gray of the others. He stares at it, then slowly walks forward, places his hand on the railing he flipped over, keeping his body stiff and far from it.

"Are you all right?" I ask.

He nods. "I know it was a freak accident, and I'm not the type to have irrational fears, really. It just . . . remember how I said it was like the ocean sucked the music out of me?"

"Yes. You found it again, though, when you went to the shore."

"I . . ." He pauses a long time. "I feel like it didn't just take something from me, it put something in my head, too. Like now the ocean is in me all the time. I can't escape it."

I don't know what to say—that sounds like something Naida would tell me.

Jude looks from where we're standing to the water, to the

church, and back again. "How did you do it, anyway?" he asks. There's nothing accusatory in his voice, but my heart speeds up a little.

"What?" I feign ignorance.

"Save me. You made it from here, down the pier, down to the shore, and then you swam out for me in the dark. I swear, I remember being at the bottom of the ocean. I didn't realize how big a distance you had to cover till now, to be honest. How'd you do it? Do you have superpowers?" he tries to joke, but the words aren't entirely teasing.

My mind formulates a dozen lies, then lies to support those lies, then lies to support those lies. I build a masterpiece of falsities in a matter of heartbeats, ready to share. *The water brought you closer to shore. I was already farther down the dock. I know the path to the church well enough to run it. The moon was bright enough that I could see you in the water.*

"There was someone else."

I say it aloud so easily, so simply, that I can't believe it. The words sit in the air, float up gently like smoke. Jude turns to me, eyes a little wide, like he's certain he heard me wrong.

I can't take back what I said, so I move forward.

"There was someone else, but first I couldn't tell you about her, and then it felt like it was too late to tell you...."

"Who is she? Wait, what happened?" Jude asks, alarmed. He doesn't sound angry, exactly, but something closer to hurt.

"It's crazy," I say quietly. I get closer, stand beside him near the railing. "If I tell you, you have to believe me."

"Of course."

I inhale. "When you fell, I did run down the path, to the shore. But you're right; it took ages. When I got to the edge of the water, there was already someone with you, swimming you out."

He looks down, like he's trying to reconcile the truth with what he's believed for weeks now. Jude shakes his head and looks back up at me.

"But the people at the hospital told me it was you. *You* told me it was you—"

"I rode with you in the ambulance, but it was another girl who pulled you out of the water." My voice sounds dead—my voice sounds like Lo's.

"You lied?"

He sounds betrayed, hurt, angry, a strange tone, too serious for the Jude I know. But I nod.

"Who?" he asks.

I inhale. "This is the part you have to believe." He's going to think I'm crazy. He's going to think I've lost it, that I'm not who he thought I was. He's going to leave. "It was Naida."

"Your friend Naida?"

"That's the night I met her, too. She was in the water."

"Swimming?"

"Sort of."

"What do you mean?" he asks.

"That's where she lives."

Jude stops, looks at me. Yes, he thinks I'm crazy, I'm a liar, I'm doing this on purpose. I don't need Jane's power to tell me all that. I look down.

231

"She lives in the water. And she can't leave the beach."

"Brown hair?" Jude suddenly says. I nod. He looks out over the ocean. His voice grows soft, his eyes almost close. "I remember her. She sang to me."

I nod again. Tears are hot in my eyes. *I wish it had been me. I'm sorry. I wish it wasn't a lie that I was the one who saved you.*

He looks up sharply at the ocean, turns to me. "Does she have a sister?"

The question throws me; I stumble to answer. "Um, yes. Or she says she does, anyway. That there are more like her."

"Named Lo?"

I feel like I've been punched in the chest. Questions, fears push around my heart, rearrange my lungs. I slowly, slowly shake my head, answer before Jude can speak again. "That's not her sister. That's her other name."

"Her other name?"

"When she was human, her name was Naida. Now her name is Lo. Lo is really the one who saved you, I guess."

"She's the girl on the beach," he whispers, turning back to look out over the water. "That explains it. She never leaves, she looks strange, she loves the water...."

"You..." *You met her? You know her? You remember her?* What question do I want to ask first? Which one do I least want the answer to?

"When I went back to the water the first time, at night, there was a girl there. And when I looked at her, I felt music again, and she sang.... It was like all these songs went into my head, everything the ocean took...." He's rambling, putting the pieces together as he speaks them aloud. Tears, more tears, though now I'm not sure for whom. He's met with Lo, with this beautiful girl, and not told me? And the song, the song—

"It was about her. The song you played for me," I say dully. *And in the shadow of a temple, where the ocean finds its prey, / That's where she's waiting for me, by the water, by the waves.* Jude's eyes shoot up, like he forgot I was standing there. He shakes his head but doesn't look apologetic.

"It was about both of you...sort of."

That doesn't help.

"Why didn't you tell me the truth?" he finally asks.

"Why didn't you tell me you knew Lo?" I answer, trying to breathe through the thick feeling in my throat. "At least I have a reason. I didn't think I'd see you again. I didn't think it'd matter, and I didn't think I could explain how this girl pulled you out of the water and then went back *into* the water. And then I didn't want you to think I was crazy, and then it felt like it'd been so long I couldn't tell you...."

"You could have told me. There were dozens of times you could have told me," he says.

"You could have talked to me, too. And you kept quiet for no reason, just to keep her a secret, just to see both of us...and so did she. You both lied to me. I saved your life, I helped her, and you both..." All I can think about right now is Jude on the beach with Lo.

I want to scream at everyone.

233

"It isn't like that," Jude mutters, shaking his head.

"Then why not tell me about her?" I ask.

"Because..." But he doesn't have an answer. He puts his fingers to his temples. "This is so much. What *is* she?"

"I thought she was my friend. And I thought you were my boyfriend."

"I am," Jude says, finally cracking. He sounds exasperated, and his mouth forms a straight line. "But you didn't tell me any of this. You think I would have cared that you had help saving me?"

"It's her you remember from that night. Not me. So yes."

"Where is she now?"

My eyes widen. I feel like I've been cut. I turn to the ocean. "Out there. Somewhere. Good luck." An announcement over the Pavilion's loudspeaker tells us that the rides and pier are closed.

"She didn't tell me she knew you. No one told me anything." He steps away from the railing, turns in a circle. "I've got to get out of here," he says darkly, exhaling. He jogs off the pier, guitar bouncing on his back. I glare at him as he goes, fold my arms, and clench my jaw.

I guess I'll be walking home.

CHAPTER THIRTY-THREE

Lo

This is my last night alive.

The moon is bright; I'll need to stay in the shadows, if he's here.

Maybe I should have stayed down below, with my sisters. The hurricane is coming. I doubt I'll survive it in the depths; I certainly won't up here. But I have a few hours, just a few… maybe that's enough. The pain in my feet when I climb from the water is strangely sweet this time—it reminds me that I'm alive, the same way the ocean did when I first got here. I look at the trail of blood behind me.

It's smaller than before, like I've merely nicked myself instead of like I've been stabbed. I close my eyes, force myself to breathe in the thick, heavy air. I remember how the old one ran from the water. There was no blood. How she ran to the thing that turned me, the thing with the scars on its chest, the monster, man, demon.

I swallow, turn, and move to tug the dress from just inside the church door. It's stiff from absorbing salt water and sitting outside for ages. Ages? No, I haven't been meeting with Celia that long. Or have I? So many of my sisters go through three or four new names before becoming old. I can't believe I'm only going to be Lo. I drop the dress. I don't care about it anymore. I only put it on to be Naida, anyway.

I don't think he's coming—he'd be here already. I lie on my back, just close enough to the water that it brushes up against my bare toes. The old one who just turned, she was kind. She was nice. I remember her from when I first came, tiny lingering memories of her telling me to stop crying, helping me braid my hair, teaching me the words to our songs. Will anyone remember me at all? I wonder if Sophia remembers Naida....

A slamming sound from behind me—I sit up, whip my head around. There's a car parked at the top of the path, bright red and so shiny the moonlight bounces off the hood. I'm not sure how I didn't notice it when I first emerged. A figure walks around the side; I prepare to run into the water. But no, the gait, it's familiar.

It's Jude. I rise.

Hands in his pockets, he comes down the path slowly, running every few steps to balance himself on the shifting sand. He doesn't have his guitar, I notice, surprised at how that makes me sad. Perhaps it's for the best; as happy as his music made me, I probably couldn't resist singing to him right now. And I wouldn't want to drown him.

He walks across the shore, doesn't lift his eyes to me until he's only a few yards away. They glint in the light.

"Hello," I say.

"Hello," he says, inhaling. "Naida."

"That's not my name," I tell him, unable to disguise the misery in my voice. How does he know her name? With him I'm Lo. With him I *like* being Lo.

"It is," he says, and he sounds something between accusatory and hurt. "Why didn't you tell me?"

"Because that's not my name," I repeat. "It used to be, a long time ago. It won't ever be Naida again. She'll be as good as dead soon."

"Don't play games," he says, and there's an unfamiliar snap to his voice. "Why didn't you tell me about Celia? And what you are? You let me think you were..."

"Normal?" I fill in the blank, motioning to my body as evidence of just how normal I'm not.

"I knew you weren't," Jude mutters, as much to himself as to me. "I knew something was strange. You don't talk like a normal girl, you don't look like a normal girl. At the ocean at midnight..."

I raise an eyebrow. "Then why did you keep coming to see me?"

He shakes his head, looks at the sand. "Because you made me remember music."

"Why couldn't Celia do that?"

"I don't know," he says. He waits. "You saved me. With her."

"Yes," I admit.

"You live in the ocean."

"Yes."

"What are you?"

"Nothing," I say. "I used to be a girl on land. And for a little while longer, I'll be a girl in the water. But soon, I'll be nothing. You can forget me. Everyone else will." *Except Celia*, I realize. She lives in the past. The thought is calming, comforting. Celia will remember me, Celia will remember Naida.

"I don't..." He presses his lips together, looks to the stars. "I don't want that to happen."

"There's nothing to be done," I say. "I can't be anything but nothing."

"You saved my life," Jude repeats, like he's convincing himself. "I'll help you. There has to be something that I can do."

I pause, look at him curiously. There was hope in his voice, pleading. He doesn't want me to go, even though he doesn't know me. I take a step away from him, surprised, alarmed, even.

He's known me for longer than other boys, though. Longer than the first boy I killed.

"Can I help? At all?" he says. His voice is barely loud enough to reach me over the sound of the waves.

I watch for an instant longer before speaking. "Do you love me?"

I didn't mean to ask, but I don't regret it. I want to know. I have to know.

238

Jude looks at me for a long time, like he doesn't understand. Not like he's scared, even though he probably should be. Because if the answer is yes, I could kill him. Something in my chest spirals through me. I think about the way it would feel to pull him in. I wonder how it would feel for his soul to become mine.

I squeeze my hands into fists, try to stop thinking about the old one, about darkness, about all the things that I could stop from happening if he loves me. I'd still vanish, but Naida would live. A tiny, good part of me would live instead of drying up on the shore like just another sea creature. I got over drowning the first boy. I could get over drowning Jude. There'd be nothing to do but get over it, with my soul intact. Naida would go on, back to her house, her sister, her dog. Her life.

And yet I know, without the tiniest hint of doubt, that I will not let myself kill Jude if he loves me. That the tiny voice inside me that wants to steal his soul will not win. I won't kill him.

I can't kill him.

But I want so, so badly for him to love me nonetheless. I step forward, reach a hand out to him. He doesn't back away, so my fingertips find his. I let my hand slide up his arm, to his shoulder. *Love me. Please, say you love me. Give me this one tiny thing before I die.*

Jude stiffens. He looks down at my hand against his skin, milky-blue on tan. Closes his eyes for a moment, then finally looks back up at me. "I'm sorry, Lo."

"Sorry?" I ask, stepping closer, trying to ignore the tight feeling in my chest, like it's full of knots.

"I think I'm in love with Celia."

I know.

"But . . . what does that have to do with me helping you?" he says.

It's not fair. She wouldn't have even met him if it weren't for me. She wouldn't know anything. I saved him. I'm the one who pulled him from the water. I stopped Molly. I walked on the shore like it didn't hurt so he would see me as a girl instead of a monster.

He should love me.

I grimace, my hands itch, ache. *Drag him into the water. Pull him in, make him regret it, make him love you.* The voice isn't mine, it isn't me, but I can feel it feeding off the sorrow that's eating up my chest.

I take a step back. My hands are shaking. *He should love me. It's not fair.*

"Lo?" he says, takes a step toward me, toward the water.

Grab his arm. You're stronger than him, especially once you hit the water. Pull him down. Maybe he's lying. Maybe he loves you. You won't know until he's gone and his soul is yours. Just because the angels aren't real doesn't mean this isn't—the old ones have told stories. They've known girls who won their souls back. It would work; it would be easy to pull him in—

"Stop," I say, taking another step back. *Don't kill him, don't kill him, don't kill him. You don't want to kill him.* The

240

voice in my head sounds like Naida one moment, Lo the next. I lean forward. He's so close. It would be easy.

He looks at the water behind me and freezes. He's afraid—of me or the water, I can't tell which. Good. I look at him, spend one second memorizing every feature I can. Then turn around and sprint toward the waves. Jude is shouting after me, yelling my name—*My name, Lo, not Naida; he's calling for Lo*—but I run faster. Drops of blood spray my calves; I don't care. If I don't leave now I'll take him, I know I'll take him, and I won't be any different from the old one on the shore. My first murder was out of desperation. If I kill again, it will be out of . . .

Nothing. What the old ones are always looking at.

The water welcomes me. The waves are rough and thrash me around. I let them. I hate Celia, I hate Jude, I hate how they'll have beautiful, happy lives, maybe together, maybe not. But either way, they won't long for their lost souls. They won't become darkness. They won't be forced to kill themselves.

Forget Lo. Forget Naida. Forget Jude, and Celia. Forget it all.

Find nothing.

CHAPTER THIRTY-FOUR

Celia

Anne and Jane are standing outside my door, whispering to each other.

"Should we call him?"

"Don't be stupid. That won't help," Anne snaps.

"Ugh. Celia? Please let us in," Jane calls through the door. "I know you're mad, but *come on*. This is, like...what sisters are *for*."

I don't want to see them any more than I want to see Jude, to be honest. I'm angry at all of them.

Anne and Jane retreat, though I hear them mumbling to each other from the kitchen. Just when I'm wondering if it's possible to sneak to the bathroom and take the world's longest bath without them catching me, I hear a knock at the front door. Swift, quiet, like the person is hoping no one will answer. Anne and Jane fall silent; I hear footsteps as one walks to the door.

"Oh, hell no," I hear Anne say. The door opens swiftly, slams into the back wall.

"Is Celia here?"

Jude's voice. It sounds weak, almost frightened.

"No. She's on a date," Anne says firmly.

A long pause.

"You're lying," he says.

"You're an asshole," she replies.

"Look, I just need to talk to her. It's about Lo."

I turn on my bed, letting the blankets wrap around me. I try to beat down the frustration, the jealousy that sprung up in my chest when I heard her name.

Jane's voice now, "You're definitely not talking to her about Lo."

"It's not like that—" Jude says, but falls silent. He sighs, begins again. "Just...just tell her that Lo left. I don't think she's coming back, but I didn't know how to stop her. I'm worried."

I sit up. Lo left? Then Naida left with her.... What does he mean by "left"?

"We'll let her know," Anne says sharply.

"Okay, I just..." Jude tries. I kick my legs over the side of the bed, stand up, and grab the knob. I don't want to see him, but I don't think I have a choice. I swing open the door. Jude is standing just outside the frame, blocked from entering by Anne and Jane—they're wearing matching angry expressions, their hands planted firmly on their hips.

Jude looks at me, takes in my red eyes and streaky face.

"Celia. I—" Anne gives him a threatening look, but he continues. "I went to talk to Lo," he says slowly, and I try to pretend that hearing that doesn't bite. "She asked me if I loved her, and I said I didn't."

I don't speak.

"I went there to see if you were telling the truth, if she really did come out of the water. And then she did, and she... I don't know. But she told me that she'd be nothing soon."

Something in my stomach twists. I swallow.

"And then she went into the ocean like something was hurting her. I'm worried about her, and I don't know who else to tell, because I don't even know what she *is*."

"She's a girl," I snap, shaking my head. "She's just a girl."

That's not true. Naida was just a girl; Lo is something more.

But Naida *needs* me. If Lo is alive, Naida is in there, somewhere. Hidden, buried, down deep maybe, but there. She has a life, a whole world that she can only remember if I help her.

I move toward the door.

"What are you doing?" Anne asks in disbelief.

"Helping Naida," I say, slipping my feet into my sandals.

"She lied to you, too! She and Jude both played you, Celia—"

"No, Lo lied to me. And Jude," I say, looking at him hastily. I don't care right now, I really don't. He doesn't understand my power, he doesn't see music in me, he doesn't care. Fine. I'll deal with that later. I reach to grab the car keys from the counter, but Anne's fingers close around them before mine can.

"You can't leave, Celia," she says firmly. She's serious, her eyes are intense. "It hasn't changed. Your future. You've got to make another choice."

"Maybe this is the other choice," I mutter. I hold out my hands for the keys, but Anne is stone-faced.

"I could drive you," Jude says. I turn to look at him.

"I'll walk. I already had to do it once today, when you left me at the pier," I snap. Jude looks hurt but doesn't argue. I push past him, down the hallway, ignoring Anne's warnings about the hurricane, about my future, about everything.

I can do this alone.

CHAPTER THIRTY-FIVE

Lo

Molly looks old.

She's on the deck of the *Glasgow*, near the other old ones. Her eyes are turned to nothing, her chin lifted to the surface. She aged fast, so fast. If the hurricane doesn't take her, I'll be surprised.

Though I suppose I won't really know. I have to go to the surface for the last time soon, before the waves get so fierce that I age and turn dark. I have to go now, before it hits.

I lean under the ship's railing and let my fingers run across the white paint that bears its name, *of Glasgow*. There was at least one other word before the *of* once. . . .

I hesitate, glance around, then dig my fingers underneath the sand and coral and shells that have latched themselves onto the wood, covering up the first word. Pull, pull hard, until things scrape against my fingertips. Finally, a piece of coral breaks free. I let it fall to the sand, eagerly crane my head to see what letter lies underneath, to see the ship's full name.

But there is nothing. The sediment was so firmly latched to the wood that it seems to have taken the outermost layer with it. The remaining wood looks almost new, unpainted, unmarred by ocean creatures. The *Glasgow* gets to keep its secrets, I guess. If it remembers them.

I sigh, rise, and move toward Molly's spot by the cherubs. She looks at me warily as I lean in to whisper to her.

"I'm going to die. Do you want to come?"

Molly narrows her eyes. "I'm not dying."

"You're…letting yourself change?" I ask. It makes me shiver—but perhaps not seeing the old one change into a monster makes it easier to accept that fate.

"Absolutely not," Molly says. "They killed my sister. They did this to me. I'll never be one of them."

"Then…" I look at her blankly. "There are no mortals you can drown. They won't love you fast enough. There isn't another choice," I protest. It suddenly occurs to me why I'm fighting so hard: I may not like Molly, but I don't want to die alone.

Molly turns back to me. "Go kill yourself, Lo. I have other plans."

I back up. I don't know what to say. I turn away, glide down the edge of the *Glasgow*. I'll need to get closer to the shore before I surface, the storm is already above us this far out to sea. Swim away, go, now, before it's too late…

I turn around, look at the *Glasgow*, at my sisters. They look like part of the ship, still, hair drifting loosely around their bodies. They are beautiful, this is beautiful, we are beautiful. I wish I could stay here. Naida may not like this world, but I do, even if I was brought here against my will, even if it makes me strange and different and half dark. I love this world.

I lift my fingers to a wave, part my lips slightly, and say good-bye.

Just go. Go now, before you change your mind.

I hurry along the ocean's floor, then up, up to where the waves are stronger, readying themselves for the storm. The water moves so easily around me sometimes, but now it is hard, hands shoving me back and forth. I feel something near my chest shudder. I could let go. Just let go, let the waves take me, let the storm change me . . .

No. Be brave.

I break the surface and look away from the nearby shore, back over the ocean. The storm is coming, black clouds racing over rocky seas. *Get on the sand, quick, before the heart of the storm reaches you—*

"Lo!"

I spin around in the water to see Key staring at me, eyes wide, lips strangely curled into the slightest of smiles.

"What are you doing here?" I ask, moving closer to her.

"Molly told me, she told me what you're planning to do. You can't die, Lo. We're almost there. We'll be angels together. We can let this storm change us."

"Key . . ." I don't want to say it, but I have to—I need to. "Key, we don't become angels. We become the same monsters that took our human lives from us. The monsters that made us ocean girls."

Key is silent for a long time. I feel the storm growing closer, the tugging at my heart getting stronger.

"Angels, monsters . . . maybe they're the same thing," Key finally says. Her voice is small but firm. I will not change her mind. I will not convince her of anything.

It's my choice to die; I suppose it's Key's choice to live as something dark. I open my mouth, try to find something to say as waves lift us up, down, stronger and stronger.

And then I hear my name. Wait, no. Not my name. Naida's name.

Key and I look to the shore, to the church. I tilt my head—someone's coming down the path, long blond hair, running—Celia.

Why is she here? I betrayed her, met with Jude, kept it a secret, longed for him to love me instead of her. I've hurt everyone. I sink down a bit and swim closer, so I can see her better, still far enough out in the water that human eyes couldn't spot me. Her face is red, her hair messy, being whipped around in the wind. I turn to look back over the ocean. . . . The storm will be here soon. She should leave, go home, go to Jude. She doesn't understand how precious the choice to be happy is. She calls out—I swim closer to hear, stay almost submerged. . . .

"Naida!" The name is almost lost in the wind. "Lo! Please!"

Maybe she wants to yell at me. To tell me she hates me, to tell me she's sorry she ever helped me. I'd deserve it, I suppose, but that doesn't mean I want to hear it. I should go. I turn—

"She's here for you?" Key asks.

"Yes," I say.

Key looks at me, confused. "You said you were meeting the boy...."

"I was," I say. "But also her."

Key looks hurt at the lie. She dips under the water for a moment, reemerges looking relieved to have wet her face again. She licks the salt from her lips. "You didn't have to lie to us. Any of us."

"I did. Or I'd have ended up exiled like Molly."

"Molly wanted to be exiled. She didn't want to be one of us. Maybe you don't, either."

"That's not true," I say. "Not true at all. I love being with our sisters. It's just Naida..."

"That's your name? Who you used to be?" Key asks. I nod. Key considers this for a moment, then looks toward Celia. "You want to go back. You should go to her."

"No. She's angry with me, too. I've ruined everything. I guess it doesn't matter though," I say, stomach tightening. "I'll be gone soon enough."

"Not if you get a soul."

"But I won't. He...he doesn't love me. And even if he did..." I feel warm water against my face—tears, not the ocean....

"He might not. But..." Key lifts my chin with her fingers, then points to the shore, "*she* came here for you."

"What do you mean?"

"That's closer to mortal love than we've seen in a long time, since before we came here. Even if she's angry, why come all this way if she doesn't care?"

I stare.

I turn, look to the shore. Celia is still calling my name, her voice cracking from straining. She's here for me. Here in a hurricane, here after I lied to her, after I lied about Jude.

You can have her soul.

"No!" I snap aloud, to Key, to myself, to Naida. I look back at Key, shake my head. "No. No, I won't."

"It's the only way out," Key says, eyes widening, like I must not understand.

"No," I say, whisper. Close my eyes, try to drown out the voice inside me, the voice that sounds like Naida clawing to get out, desperate, longing to live again. *No. No.*

"Lo, the storm will be here soon. I don't want you to die. You have to—"

"I'd rather die," I say, but my voice shakes. I'm afraid to look at the shore again. Afraid if I see Celia, something will change my mind.

"You can be human again. Don't throw this away," Key says, grabbing my shoulders. "Please, Lo. It's too late for the rest of us, but you have a choice—"

"This isn't a choice. It's murder," I hiss. I wince as I hear Naida's name bounce across the waves again.

My name is Naida Kelly. I have an older sister. We lived in a house surrounded by trees. My feet didn't bleed when I walked on land, and my skin wasn't milky-blue. I was a nor-mal girl.

I duck back into the water, try to breathe slowly. No. My name is Lo. I live in the ocean with dozens of sisters. We were once human, but that's gone. It's gone, and it's never coming back. I can't take a soul. I won't take a soul. I can't...

My name is Naida Kelly.

I close my eyes. Fight it. Fight, fight... Naida's voice grows louder, louder, till she's screaming in my head.

My name is Naida Kelly, and I want to live again.

CHAPTER THIRTY-SIX

Naida

My sister did whatever she could to save me.

I have to do the same.

Whatever it takes.

CHAPTER THIRTY-SEVEN

Celia

The wind is picking up—it isn't supposed to be the worst hurricane I've ever seen, but it's still to the point where I know I shouldn't be on the beach. Yet I slink through the fence by the calliope, run through the now-empty park. It's frightening, so empty, lifeless....I hurry to the pier, to the path down by the ocean. The waves are already dangerously choppy, white sea foam everywhere. The storm is close, so close....I squint, put a hand to my forehead, try to see—

Yes. There she is. Her head, her eyes just above the water, disappearing with each wave.

"Naida!"

She doesn't move, looks away from me, like she's speaking with the waves. "Naida!" I try again. "Lo! Please!"

Nothing. Naida—Lo—dips underwater, vanishes. I cry out in anger, grip my hands into fists. Naida can't be gone;

Lo can't have taken her. Not after all we've worked through, after all we've remembered together. . . . I turn around, look away from the ocean in frustration.

"Celia!"

I whip my head back toward the waves and sigh so hard that it's almost hard to catch my breath again. She's not dead. She's not dead. Naida is walking toward me, struggling against the thrashing tide. Everything is gray—the horizon, the light, the ocean, even the sand. Naida's skin is bluer than before, her eyes darker, but it's still her. She didn't give up after all. Jude was wrong.

"Jude came to me. He told me you were gone, that Lo . . ."

"No," Naida says, smiling. She shakes the water from her hair. "No, I'm all right. I . . ." She looks away. "I should have told you Lo was meeting with him. I didn't always remember it. I'm sorry."

"You should have. He should have," I say, voice harder than I mean it to be. I shake it off. "Never mind. I was just worried. It's getting harder for you to remember. I was afraid Lo won and you were gone. . . ." I cringe as the wind whips my hair into my eyes. I need to go, I need to leave, but I'm afraid that if I turn around Naida will vanish again. I can't let that happen, not after coming this far. I squint, try to open my eyes, looking down to shield myself from the brunt of the gale.

"Your feet," I say, pointing. "They aren't bleeding."

Naida looks down, eyes wide. "You're right. It hurts but . . . not like before."

"Do you think you can leave the beach, then? Maybe it won't be as bad as last time. Maybe it's working. You're remembering," I say, almost embarrassed by how eager I sound.

Naida looks at me, presses her lips together. "No. That's not why they stopped bleeding. It's not because I'm remembering."

"It could be! Maybe you're more human now—"

"They aren't bleeding, because I'm changing. From Lo into darkness. It's happening, it's happening now."

I step back—am blown back, actually. Lightning cracks out over the sea. I can't stay here.... "We'll fight it. Tell me how to help."

Naida swallows hard, there's something she's not telling me. "Celia, I'm sorry. This shouldn't be happening. It shouldn't be me—they chose me because I once had a twin sister. That's the only reason. That made them want me, made me eligible to be their ocean...thing. That's not fair. It's not right...." She sounds broken, desperate—like Lo sounded the first time she asked me to help her remember, even though the voice is all Naida. Lightning cracks again.

"Because you had a twin once? Is that the sister I don't see in your memories?"

"I think that's her," Naida answers.

"But that means...Does that mean I could end up like Lo, if something happened to my sisters?" It sounds like I'm experimenting with the concept on my tongue. Surely no. I'm ordinary. Well, I have a power, but other than that...I couldn't become something like Lo. I think about Anne and Jane. They were right—we aren't just stuck together; we *are* stronger together. Torn apart we're . . . Naida.

Naida shrugs. "I would think losing a triplet makes you as desirable as losing a twin. I don't know. It's not fair, though. It's not right."

"I know, it isn't," I say quickly. "Look, Naida, I can't stay, but don't worry. We'll fix this. Maybe you should go into the church."

"No." She takes a step toward me, cringes.

"What?"

She takes another step toward me, so close I want to step away, but I know the wind will throw me off balance if I do. The waves are getting bigger. The storm is here—

"Naida—"

She grabs my wrist, locks her fingers tight. I stare at her skin against mine, then meet her eyes.

"I'm so sorry. I don't want to do this," she says. "But it isn't fair either way, no matter what happens."

I tug my hand, but she's strong, so, so strong. My heart starts to beat fast. I don't understand. "What are you doing? Naida, stop." My voice is panicked. Something is wrong, something is very wrong.

"It's the only way I can be Naida again. The only way we can get our souls back. We have to kill a mortal and take theirs—"

My eyes widen, tears form. "What? Naida . . . no, don't. Please," I whisper, though the words mostly get caught in my throat. The sea thrashes, threatens us, a monster held back by the sand. "You do have a choice. You always have a choice with the future. No matter what happened in the past. You're my friend."

Naida stares, motionless despite the fact that I'm pulling hard, trying to run, trying to yank my wrist away. Even now, her memories are cycling through my head: moments with her sister, at school, learning to drive, everything happy and beautiful—wrong against the eyes of the girl I see in front of me. She won't kill me; surely the girl from a little town won't kill me. She can't; she doesn't have it in her.

But she's desperate.

You can't trust someone that desperate.

She was the desperate one all along.

I scream when she pulls me toward the water. I dig my heels into the sand, throw my weight backward, but she drags me, like she's part of the current. I've seen her swim—I'll never survive in the waves. I know that, but there's nothing I can do except scrape along the sand. There's nothing here to grab on to, nothing to hold me back. My skin is turning purple under Naida's hands. She's marching forward—

And then we're in the water.

She is strong, so incredibly strong. Her hair flies over my face as we push through the first set of waves. She isn't Lo, though, she's still clumsier in the water than her counterpart. She has to let go of my wrist for a moment; I try to scramble away, but the waves toss me, flip me under. Water shoots into my lungs, sand and salt fill my eyes. I don't know which way the shore is, where Naida is—she grabs my wrist again.

Lightning, thunder. The rain begins, so heavy and thick that it splashes more water up from the ocean. The waves are rough; the sand they toss around stings my arms—we're almost into deep water, though we're moving slowly now that the waves try to push us to shore. I kick hard at Naida's legs; they buckle for a moment, I feel her grip loosen, but I can't get the same force behind my muscles in the water as I can on land. It's only a moment before her grip is tighter than ever. I think I feel my wrist breaking from the pressure.

We make it to the sandbar, begin to cross over into the deep water. This is it. It'll be over soon. I have to do something.

"Naida, please!" I sputter, hacking as a wave fills my mouth with seawater. "Don't, please don't," I beg, plead. "Think about your sister, about Sophia. Your dad. They wouldn't want this."

"They'd want me to survive. They fought for me to survive," she says over the hissing noise of rain on the ocean. She takes a few more steps; the sandbar drops off quickly. It's only a second before the water is up past my waist again.

No, no. In the deep water I won't stand a chance—I have to get away. I reach forward, grab a handful of her hair, and yank, twisting as I do so. Naida shrieks but doesn't stop, not even when the fistful comes away in my fingers. I claw at her arm, try to wrap my forearm around her neck, but she's slick and moves around me. She's in control. We start down the sandbar, I'm standing on my toes just to keep my head out of the water, and then, then...

Nothing. I can't reach the ocean floor. I gasp as wave after wave knocks me under. I can't swim with her holding on to me. She lets go, but it's all I can do to keep myself above water, all I can do to prepare myself for her to pull me down. No, wait. She's looking at something, toward the shore. Between swells, almost obscured by the heavy sheets of rain, I finally see what she's looking at.

Jude. On the beach. He sees us. He's yelling. He's pacing. He's afraid. Up by the top of the pier, the car's headlights beam through the rain, and I make out two forms like mine—Anne and Jane.

I want to tell all three of them to run. But Jude is getting into the water. I look at Naida; she turns back to me.

Then she lurches forward and pushes me under.

CHAPTER THIRTY-EIGHT

I am lost. I'm here, but I'm lost, like I'm watching through someone else's eyes instead of my own.

I see myself grabbing Celia's shoulders. Forcing her head under the water. She fights, struggles, but she's no match for me, not here where it's deep. I swim down, down. Her eyes widen, and she's forced to release the breath she's been holding. The air floats past me in bubbles, and Celia inhales the ocean water.

I can't control my body. I'm trapped, watching as Celia's eyes drift shut, as her body jerks, uselessly trying to siphon oxygen from the water.

I scream at myself, will my hands to stop, fight, fight, fight, but there's nothing I can do, nothing I can change. Naida is in control.

The wind picks up, the seas toss us. The motion snaps

Celia awake for a moment, a tiny moment; she tries to kick toward the surface but fails. She won't make it, she won't live....

Help her.

I scream, force my way to the front of my mind, reach down, and grab Celia's hand. We're deep, the surface is far away, and I can already feel Naida clamoring to regain power over the body we share. Come on, so close, if I can just get her up, yes—we break the surface of the water, only to be knocked aside by the waves. Still, at least she's out. I grab Celia's shoulders, hold her head out of the water, try to turn her away as wave after wave strike us, as the rain intensifies. Everything looks gray. I can't see—

Jude, yes. Jude, he's trying to swim to us. He's struggling, and the water batters him around, but he forges through the waves anyhow. Naida is screaming, shouting, clawing her way into my head. *Just get Celia to Jude, get her to Jude,* I think. I move toward him, he sees us, he sees me. His eyes are the same gray as everything else—

Drown her. Take her soul.

And suddenly I'm pushed away again, hidden within my own body, like I'm watching a dream. I try to dive again with Celia, though my body doesn't move as easily in the water now that Naida controls it. Hurry, Jude, hurry—

He's here, he reaches us. The waves throw us apart for a moment, toss Celia's body away from me. Jude sees, and we race for her, arms outstretched. His clothes weigh him down, but he's closer. He grabs her left arm as I grab her right. I hiss at him, lash out to strike him, but he dodges down in the water, kicks back up to the surface. His arm is drawn back. He punches at my face—contact. Pain explodes by my eye. I feel warm blood against the cold rain, but I'm back, Naida is gone again. I release Celia, hold my hands where Jude can see them.

"No, it's me. It's not Naida, it's me!" I shout, but Jude doesn't seem to understand. I shake my head; waves throw him and Celia under for a moment. Her head lolls to the side—she has to breathe, she needs air, she needs to get to land now. I start toward her, but Jude shouts, draws his hand back again, ready to hit me. Lightning crashes behind him. The wind picks up, blows us along the waves, toward the end of the pier.

It isn't fair. Naida's voice, rippling through me. *I'm not supposed to be you. Let me have her.*

She's right. She's right, and I feel her voice aching, her fury, her sorrow, as she pushes forward in my mind again. I dive at Jude, shove him away, wrap my elbow around Celia's neck. Down, down, pull her down. I can feel Celia's soul—feel it. She's dying, and it will be mine. It's golden and bright, like the sun, like joy, something that I think will light me if I swallow it. The deeper I push her, the more I can feel it leaving her body, drifting from her lips and surrounding me. It'll be easy.

"Lo!"

My name, my name, not Naida's, called from above. I look up. Jude is underwater; he let the last of his air from his

263

lips to shout my name. His hair and clothes float around his body. He swings back and forth in the waves. He's not leaving her. He's not leaving her. He's not leaving me.

I don't want to end this life as a killer, but I realize now: Someone has to die.

I scream.

I'm so sorry, Naida.

I fight my way back to my own head. *My name is Lo. I have dozens of sisters. I live underwater. My feet bleed when I walk on land, but I know beauty under the waves better than any human. I used to be a girl, but now I am this.*

My name is Naida Kelly.

No. No. My name is Lo.

Snapping back into my mind is like waking up suddenly. I'm here, I'm here. I close my lips and stop screaming. Grab Celia and jet toward the surface. I burst through the ocean's ceiling, swim for the shore, go, go, faster—she needs air. Jude is behind me, swimming slowly, but I don't have time to wait for him to catch up.

The rain is blinding. It's almost like still being under-water, but I make it to the sandbar, then to the shallows. She'll make it, she has to make it. Celia's body is limp in my arms as I clamber from the waves toward the shore—or what's left of it. The bottom of the church is underwater; the waves lap at the edge of the path up to the pier. I can't leave her within the water's reach. Celia's head lolls back, her hair drips, eyes stay closed. I can feel the wound from Jude hitting me still bleeding, running down the side of my face. I dash up the pathway, to the edge of the pier. My feet burn, but I push forward through the shut-down rides and booths. Finally, finally I set Celia down by the calliope, as far from the water as I dare go.

I feel sick, dizzy. I want to go back to the ocean but no, no. Celia doesn't move; her chest isn't rising. I need to go get Jude, help him out of the water, but I'm afraid to leave her. I close my eyes, try to think back to when Celia and I were saving him. I pressed on his chest, yes, I can do that—I reach forward, pump my hands down on Celia's chest for a moment. Something needs to happen, something has to happen. I lean down toward her face, listen for breath. Nothing.

She put her mouth up to Jude's, I remember. I can try...I can try, but I'm afraid. I'm afraid that will wake Naida—that's how we're supposed to take souls, with a kiss. It's not a kiss, but it's close enough, enough that I'm frightened....

I have to try, though. I hear shouting near me, ignore it. She has to live, she has to—

I press on Celia's chest again, again, then lean over, press my mouth against hers and exhale. Breathe, please breathe.... I brace myself, waiting to hear Naida's voice, waiting for her to cast me aside....

She doesn't.

But Celia breathes.

CHAPTER THIRTY-NINE

Celia

I cough, gag. Water erupts from my throat and spills down my neck. I'm cold. I feel beaten, like my body is nothing but bruises. But air—I can breathe, I can breathe. I turn on my stomach, and more water pours from my lungs; I force a breath in. Another, another. I'm out of the water, I'm out, I'm alive. Jude pulled me out; he got to me in time.

I can't believe I'm alive.

I turn onto my back again, panting, too tired to move; my eyes drift over and—

She's here, watching me with dark eyes. It wasn't Jude who pulled me out; it was her. I can't feel my limbs, but I try to back up; I push myself across the pavement, into a wall—the calliope, I realize, when I look to the side and see paintings of trees and birds. The little bit of effort leaves me winded, exhausted. When I look up, she's holding up her palms, a surrender.

"It's all right," she says, framed by the Ferris wheel behind her, like it's some sort of halo.

"Lo." I can tell by her voice, by her eyes now that I look closer—

Feet pounding on pavement—I look up to see Anne and Jane running toward me, hair whirling around them in the wind, eyes wild and angry. They don't slow as they look from me to Lo, though their eyes widen at either her skin color or her nudity. I don't have time to work out which it is—Jane runs, drops down beside me, and Anne charges into Lo, knocking her to the pavement. They collapse together; the concrete cuts them both up, but Anne is to her feet almost instantly with blood running from both knees.

"Get away from her!" Anne shouts. "Jane, get her out of here!" Lo looks like a caged animal, crouched to the ground while Anne looms over her. Anne's hands are drawn into fists, her eyes serious. Jane hauls me to my feet; I stumble and hear Anne shout again, Lo make some sort of hissing sound in response—

"Stop!" I shout. Jane freezes. Anne doesn't take her eyes off Lo to look back at me. "Stop." *Breathe, just breathe.* "She saved me."

"She tried to drown you. We saw the whole thing from up by the pier."

"It was Naida," Lo says, voice fallen as she presses against the wall, wary of Anne's fury.

"Where is Naida now?" I ask weakly, coughing as yet

267

more water forces its way from my lungs. Anne turns to look at me, baffled, but says nothing.

"She's gone," Lo answers.

"Gone?" I meet her eyes; she swallows, nods. Lightning crashes, and the wind whistles through the rides. I can hear the waves, wonder how much of the shore they've consumed. . . . I close my eyes for a moment.

Gone. She's gone. It doesn't seem real.

"Will someone explain what's happening?" Anne snaps, looking from me to Lo. Jane's still holding on to my arms with a death grip; I shake her off.

"It's fine. It wasn't her who tried to kill me. It was the other girl . . . in her head." Saying that sounds just as stupid as I thought it would.

"How do you know she isn't lying?" Anne says darkly, glaring back toward Lo. Lo's eyes flicker dangerously as Anne leans a little too close. I inhale, hold my breath—Anne's anger pitted against Lo's strength isn't something I want to see.

"I . . . I can tell. I can't explain it—"

"I don't trust her. I know what I saw," Anne says, unconvinced. She looks from me and Jane to the fence behind the calliope, where I realize our car is sitting, headlights still on.

"Let me go or Jude will die," Lo says suddenly, voice dark. We stare at her; her face is steady. "He was swimming behind me, but he isn't here yet. He must still be in the water."

I inhale, panic, look at Anne. "Let her go!"

"How do I know she won't try to kill you again?" Anne snaps.

"I..." I don't know. I just believe she won't. And that's not going to be enough for my sisters.

"I can tell," Jane says shortly. She glances at me, rises. Jane trades places with Anne; my sisters look at each other warily, have a silent conversation I'm not let in on. Jane extends a hand to Lo. Lo looks at me, back to Jane, eyes cautious but daring. Finally, she reaches up, holds out her palm. Jane cringes as she lays her fingertips on Lo's blue-toned skin. Anne tenses as Jane inhales, waits a moment, then draws her hand back.

"She doesn't want to kill us. Any of us. She wants to save Jude. She loves him—" She stops short, glances back at me. Lo looks down, closes her eyes.

"I have to go now," she says under her breath.

"Go. Let her go!" I snap. Jane winces but finally steps back from Lo and the calliope. Lo leaps to her feet, moves to bolt, then turns—

"If I change, Celia, if I go dark...be careful. Don't trust me." She looks from me to my sisters. "Remember what I said about twins?" She looks from me to my sisters grimly as I nod. "Triplets are even better." She swiftly turns, sprints down the pier, and dives off the side, like we've set her free. I rise as she's falling. *Please find him, please find him—*

"What did she mean?" Anne asks, but Jane interrupts before I can answer.

"And who are they?" Jane asks, pointing to the other side

of the Ferris wheel. I narrow my eyes against the rain and look up.

Moving toward the base of the pier, gazing out over the water, are people. A dozen or so, maybe more. The girls are tall and willowy, with long hair and sharp faces. The men are muscular and bare-chested. They watch the ocean like it's telling them something, like it knows secrets they want. The man in front turns slightly to talk to the others, and even through the rain, I can see something on his chest. Rows and rows of scars, thick like the side of my hand and raised up off the skin.

Naida's memories rear up in my head, trample through my mind.

I couldn't forget this memory, the memory that ended in screaming, the memory that Naida buried deep down inside her. It's them.

The monsters that changed her.

CHAPTER FORTY

Lo

It's hard even for me to move in the waves—no wonder Jude couldn't make it out. I see him ahead, hurry forward, wincing as stray boards from the pier knock against me in the surf. I feel something stir in my core, something that wants to change, wants to let the storm take me away....

No. No, I'm not done here. I have to save Jude. Faster, faster, swim faster. He's slowing down, the storm is slowing me down—as much as the water is a part of me, the storm still makes it almost impossible to swim. Come on, a little farther, I'm almost there. Then suddenly there's a head next to his, rising out of the water, hair still red enough to look like poison against the gray waves.

Molly.

Thunder crashes, ripples through me. She's going to kill him, I can feel it—

No. She swims past him, rushes to the shore. Is she changing? Was that her plan? I'm about to call for her when a flash of movement on the pier catches my eye. Dozens of people, standing by the base of the pier. Mostly men, but some girls. Girls I once knew, ocean girls. Demons, darkness, evil. They stare at us, smiling, watching, waiting. Waiting for us to turn. Waiting for us to join them. In front of them all is the monster—the man, he looks like a man now. He's shirtless, muscular, perfect, save the thick axelike scars on his chest.

He looks at me over the pier railing—right *at* me, as if he were inches away.

And he smiles.

I can't breathe. A wave roars over me, punches me underwater; for a moment everything feels black and hazy, then I feel a hand wrap around my wrist. Another on my shoulder, steadying me, holding me still against the ocean. I blink, wait for my vision to clear. Key. It's Key. And she's changed—or is *changing*. Her eyes are different, her face is different—she looks like a girl who merely resembles my friend.

"He's there," she calls over the sound of the rain, so loud it's deafening even underwater. She points behind me; I see Jude's body sinking slowly. "Go save him."

"Key, you...you're..." What do I say?

"I'm turning. Leaving the ocean behind," Key says, and she smiles at me, a dangerous type of smile. "It's what I want. What I've always wanted."

"But you'll be a...monster."

"Look at us. We're all monsters anyhow. There's no choice," Key says. She inhales, looks in the direction of the pier. "Come with me, Lo. Save him, let him go, but then come with me. It's where you belong."

I shake my head, but the storm is pulling at me once again. I could go. I could save Jude, leave him on the shore to Celia and her sisters. Just because Lo has to die doesn't mean a new version of me can't be born tonight. I'd be with Key, I'd be with my other changed sisters.

Don't give in. Don't give in. Don't change.

I feel darkness flickering through me, licking at the space around my heart.

CHAPTER FORTY-ONE

❧

Celia

It's him, it's him and he's here for them, for Naida—Lo—for her sisters.

And if he sees my sisters and me? Then he's here for us, too.

"Hide," I say swiftly. "Now, hide."

Anne and Jane aren't used to taking orders from me, but I suppose I sound so panicked they don't question it—we jump behind the calliope, peer through the pipes at the people.

No, not people. I don't know what they are, but they aren't human. Some could pass, yes, but others have too-long teeth, or fingers like claws. Some of the girls have white fur-like hair growing down their necks and along their spines; as we watch, it dissolves and becomes jet-black, thick and beautiful hair that reminds me of Lo's.

"What are they?" Jane whispers as lightning cracks

overhead. I glance back—the car is right there. We could get in it and go. But Jude—no, we can't leave till we have Jude.

"Celia! Seriously, what are they?" Anne asks, and for the first time in recent memory, she sounds afraid.

I shake my head. "They're what turned Lo into what she is. They're monsters. They attacked her and changed her and—" I mean to say more, but a figure appears at the edge of the pier, walking up the path. It's a girl like Lo—same blue skin, same features, naked and dripping wet. One of her sisters. I wince as they look at her and smile, and the scarred one holds his hand out. *Run, run.* I want to scream for her to run, but I know she won't. Why would she? She's so clearly one of them, being welcomed by them, just like Lo described.

The scarred man wraps his fingers in hers, but it's not loving—it's controlling, like he's claiming her as his own. And then he changes, slowly, methodically. His spine shifts, cracks loudly enough that we can hear it from our hiding spot. His skin dissolves away, leaving thick and matted fur. And his jaw—it stretches, stretches like the bones themselves are clay, elongating until it's not human anymore. Elongating until it's a wolf's jaw, a wolf's face, a wolf's yellow searing eyes. If there was any doubt that this man is the monster that changed Naida, it's gone. I close my eyes for a moment, try to keep from vomiting at the idea of fighting it, of what Naida's sister had to face.

Jane drops to the ground, weak-kneed, while Anne tightens her grip on the calliope. Together we watch the others change from human to monster—the men becoming huge,

275

dark wolves and the women becoming eerily beautiful white ones. The new girl is the last to change. It looks painful; she screams when her spine shifts and cracks. They're still tall even as beasts, with massive claws and slick teeth; I think of Naida's memory, of how it felt when the teeth popped through the skin of her chest, into her heart.

"We can't stay *here*. At least get in the car," Anne whispers urgently.

I grimace at the idea of leaving Jude. *Lo will save him. She's done it before; she won't let him die. Trust her.* I nod meekly, slowly lower myself; Anne and I each grab one of Jane's arms, hoist them over our shoulders. Just through the gate, the car is right there on the other side. We can wait for Jude, we can make it out, we'll be fine. I look down to adjust my arm under Jane—

"Celia," Anne says, voice serious, dead. I look up, then at the fence.

There's a girl, standing just a few feet from us, blocking our path. Blue-skinned, hair that looks like it might have once been red. Her eyes are different from Lo's, more human, but they're sharp and dangerous.

"You're Lo's friend," she says. Her voice is even and deep.

"Yes," I say quickly, almost relieved. Another sister, one who isn't going to the monsters. Will she help us?

"Triplets," she says, looking from me to Anne and Jane. I hesitate, but then nod again. The girl licks her lips; I can see her slightly pointed teeth flicker when she does so. She inhales; I wait, watch, feel Jane tremble beside me, then—

"Here!" she shouts, voice shooting through the rain, across the empty Pavilion—to the monsters. "Come here!"

My heart sinks, and finally, Jane really does faint. Not that it matters; the girl darts forward, shoves the three of us backward, so, so strong. We smash into the calliope and fall to the ground. I can feel I'm bleeding; everything is blurry and stings. She leans over us and pushes hard on the back of the calliope. Its ancient wheels creak but give, and it rolls to the side, revealing us, revealing the car, revealing Lo's sister to the monsters. I try to crawl to my feet, shaky, but the girl pushes me back to the ground.

I can't live like Lo. I don't want to forget.

I turn my head, squinting in the rain, force myself to look. The monsters are walking toward us slowly, methodically, still beasts. Lo's sister leans over and hisses, animal-like. She doesn't need words to make it clear that we aren't to move. Anne whimpers nearby; Jane's breathing is haggard and rough as the monsters begin to change one at a time, snouts sucking back to form human faces. The scarred one gives us a curious look, stops moving when Lo's sister tenses, steps out in front of us.

"Molly, correct?" the scarred one says after a long moment. "I remember you."

"You should," Lo's sister—Molly—says. Her voice is thick, furious. "Do you remember my sister? The one you killed?"

"Not especially," he says, grinning wickedly. Molly's hands wrap into fists, so hard I hear her knuckles crack.

There's a long pause; Molly inhales several times, like she's about to speak, but it takes several tries for the words to emerge.

"I'll make a deal," she says. "There's three of them. You'll get two new girls if you kill one, won't you?"

"We will," the man says cautiously. "But what's the deal?"

"Let me go. Release me from this . . . this life. And I'll give one of them to you to kill."

"What makes you think we can't kill one of them anyhow?" the man asks, as if this entire exchange amuses him.

"I can snap their necks before you take another step," Molly growls. "All three of them. It'll be easy. I'm strong now, stronger than I was when you killed my sister. You made me this way."

"Ah," the monster says, but I can see he thinks she has a point. He looks at me and my sisters. Anne's face is white, and there's a trickle of blood running down her jaw; Jane hardly seems awake at all, head nodding and falling back against the pavement. "They're lovely. And you're fighting changing—it'll take forever for you to join us. . . ."

"*Take one*," Molly says through gritted teeth. The monster hesitates.

He's going to do it. He's going to let her trade us.

Two of us are going to change.

I can't, I can't let it happen, no—

"Me," I sputter, realizing my mouth is full of blood. Molly glances back at me, surprised. "Me," I repeat. "Take me."

278

"Interesting," the monster muses. I hold my hands out and clamber to my feet.

"Kill me," I pant, meeting Molly's eyes. "I can't live like that in the water. I can't do it."

"What are you doing?" Anne shouts, angry, hurt, confused. She starts to rise, but Molly kicks her back down, her foot solidly planting in Anne's stomach. My sister hacks, chokes to regain her breath.

"My sister didn't get a choice," Molly says slowly. "I would have volunteered. I'd rather have died than watch her be killed—"

"I can't watch you die, Celia!" Anne sputters, still gasping for air. I look over my shoulder at her.

"I never fit in with you and Jane anyhow," I say, voice shaking. I'm sure we're both crying, but the tears blend so seamlessly with the rain that it's hard to tell. Molly looks from me to the monster, then grabs my arm.

"Her," Molly says. "You'll take her. You can have the other two. And then you let me go."

"Of course," the monster says, but his words don't reach his eyes. He's lying. He's not letting Molly go—he probably *can't* let Molly go. It's so obvious, how does she not see it? Molly takes a step forward. I cringe as I think of Naida's memory, about the man, the wolf, the beast.

Will he make it fast? I find his eyes. No. He won't.

It doesn't matter. It'll be fine. He'll kill me. He'll try to change my sisters.

But it won't work. They'll walk out of the ocean and be

able to go home. At least, I think that's the case. Because like I told Anne—I never fit in with her and Jane. I'm their not-quite-perfect replica.

I'm not identical.

If what Naida and Lo told me is true, that means it won't work. Killing me will just mean my death, not their transformation. That seems fair, really—this is my fault, all my fault. . . . I wanted to be myself, wanted to be strong, be brave. I wanted a better power, even. This is it. This is my power. Truly becoming something beyond Anne and Jane's sister. I swallow, try to stop shaking, but it doesn't work. Molly and I grow closer; her grip on my arm tightens. Is she trembling, too? Why? Closer, closer, just a few steps away . . . The monster reaches out for me, his arm transforming into something clawlike as he does. *Don't touch me, please. I don't want him to touch me*, I think uselessly. . . .

And the next thing I know, I'm back on the ground.

Molly has shoved me to the side, leaped through the air. She's on the man before he knows what's happening, her arms wrapped around his head, and then—*crack*. A bright sound, the sound of his neck breaking. His body falls to the ground, but before his chest hits the pavement, he explodes into shadows that skirt away in the rainstorm. There's screaming, growling, the snapping of spines as the men transform back into monsters. Teeth everywhere, fur, claws, saliva—they're on Molly, ripping at her skin, bright red blood staining the mouths of the white wolves. Molly doesn't stop, though. She's shrieking, furious, fighting, clawing at them with everything she has—

Anne grabs my hand, yanks me away, and suddenly we're running, around the calliope, back through the fence. Jane is slow, but we make it to the car; I dive into the driver's seat, slam the door behind me. I can hear Molly screaming.

"Go, Celia, drive!" Anne shouts, wrapping her arms around Jane's trembling body in the backseat. I snap to life, throw the car into reverse, we have to go—

Molly screams again, this time more from pain than rage.

"They're killing her," I say.

"She wanted to die, clearly," Anne answers. "Please, Celia, we can't help Jude—"

"It's not about Jude," I say. "Not right now. I have to help Molly."

"What does it matter—"

"We have to help her kill them, Anne. If they live, they'll come back for us, back for other girls. We have to help."

I look at Anne in the rearview mirror as I say it; her mouth, open and ready to argue, slams shut. She shoots her hand forward, grabs my shoulder, closes her eyes.

"The fence," she says meekly, breathlessly. "Go straight. Don't try to cut through our opening."

"We'll kill more of them that way?"

"I have no idea," she says as she reaches across Jane and buckles our sister's seat belt for her. "I can't see anything in the future right now, not under pressure like this. I don't know what I'm doing, Celia. I don't know what you're doing. But if we go through our opening, I think we'll hit the calliope."

"Got it," I say, trying to smile at her in the rearview mirror. It doesn't work. I grab my seat belt, click it into place. Turn toward the monsters. *We're stronger together, despite everything.*

I think Molly is dead—I don't hear her screaming anymore. Not that it matters. I think of Lo, of Naida, of her sister, of dead twins, and of all the girls in the ocean who are forgetting their old lives.

What good is knowing the past if you won't change the future?

I slam my foot down on the accelerator.

CHAPTER FORTY-TWO

Lo

Jude's body is heavy, like someone has tied weights to my arms and legs. His heart is beating, though—I can feel it when I hold him against me to swim, different and strange compared with the ocean's rhythm. *Make it to shore. Just get him to shore!* I shout to myself. He'll live. He has to live, I won't let him die, even if he's going to come to and tell Celia he loves her, even if he's going to think I'm a killer, if he won't believe that it was Naida who wanted Celia dead. *Just get him to shore. He has to live.*

A smaller voice, a certain voice deep down in me: *Get him to shore before you go dark and kill him.* Because despite the fact that the monsters aren't by the pier anymore, I can still feel how badly the storm wants to take me. It calls to me, it promises me strength like I've never known, it promises me the end of pain. . . .

I hear a scream just as my feet strike sand. Who was that? I don't know that voice; I don't recognize it....I wrap my arms around Jude's torso for a better grip, pull him along, hurry forward. Celia might need me, Key might need me, hurry. I crash through the sea grass at the top of the trail and set Jude down, look to see where the screaming came from, who else I can help, I can save—

I see the car just as it hits them.

It crashes into the monsters. Several fall to the ground, then become strange, dark shadows that blend in with the rain. Others run, white wolves, dark wolves, beasts that are something of both wolf and man. I look for the one who turned me, but I don't see him—is he gone? The car continues forward, crashes spectacularly into the side of a building—the arcade. The horn sounds a single, bold tone; smoke pours from the hood. I don't know where to run, what to do. I look to the car—it's Celia and her sisters. I can see their blond hair in the windows, can't tell if they're moving. Two white wolves are left and one half man-monster; I move toward them, tense. They're at the Pavilion's gate. They slow, look back at me with umber eyes.

The white wolves transform. One becomes an ocean girl I don't remember.

The other becomes Key.

But she is not Key. She's nothing resembling Key—save for the tiny, tiny bit of remorse I see on her face when she glances toward the calliope, at a body on the pavement. Molly. Her hair doesn't look red at all now compared with

284

the blood pooling with rain on her abdomen. She's dead, so clearly dead.... I grimace, turn back to Key and the others.

I don't want to kill Key, but if I have to, if she forces me, I will.

The male says something to the other two, something I can't hear. Then all three contort, change, let fur split through their skin. They become monsters again and run, out into the storm, over the road, to a grove of palmettos.

They're gone.

I hear movement behind me—Celia and one of her sisters helping Jude. His eyes are open; he's alive. I exhale a breath I feel like I've been holding forever. I want to run to them. But not yet, not yet. As they help him into the arcade through the hole in the wall the car smashed, I run in the opposite direction, to Molly's body.

It's tiny, it's broken. Raindrops bounce off her skin like she's nothing more than the tipped-over calliope or the trash that's blowing by. Her hands are torn to pieces. I can see the bones in her legs and one shoulder. I kneel, gather her up, and clutch her tight to me. She's not warm—though, really, are we ever? I rise and carry her, one foot in front of the other, toward the pier, trying to walk slowly to keep her head from tipping backward.

Molly fought them. She killed the one who turned me. She must have.

So we both planned to die today. I wish I had realized that even when it looked like I didn't have a choice, I did—I could have been brave. I could have been like her.

But I did choose. I chose not to let the storm take me. I fought it. I refused to be a monster.

I chose to be Lo.

I carry Molly's body to the edge of the pier, use one hand to smooth her hair off her pale face. I hope *something* about the angels is true. I hope she goes into the air, hope she finds her twin sister. I hope she's happy.

I release her body. It plummets into the ocean and is swallowed up almost instantly. The water continues on, churns, crashes in the storm.

I hope she's home.

EPILOGUE

There are lights at the surface, she told them over and over. *Lights unlike the sun, lights from carnivals and stars. You have to see them. You have to choose to never forget them.*

To never forget yourself.

They were afraid to believe her, though some did anyhow. Not all. *It's hard to believe something ugly over something as beautiful as angels*, she reminded herself when some of her sisters turned their backs on her, looked away when she approached.

Angels—that's what the newspapers called the triplets. Anne and Jane soaked it up, weaving stories about how they dramatically rescued Jude from the hurricane. Celia and Jude smiled, nodded, agreed, but they knew that the real story did not end at the Pavilion that evening. That it still hadn't ended.

And so they went back to the ocean.

Seven o'clock, just like always. The broken part of the fence by the calliope was patched up, but it didn't take long for the four of them to find a new entrance. The Pavilion was closed for the season, some of the rides being slowly dismantled to be repaired.

"Who will we practice on, with this place closed?" Jane asked, sighing. Jude rolled his eyes. He knew about them now—about their powers, about their secrets—but after everything with Lo, it barely rattled him.

"You won't practice on anyone!" Jude said. "It's weird!"

"We're going to see a girl who lives underwater, and *that's* what's weird?" Anne pointed out. She still didn't like Lo and wasn't convinced that the part of Lo that tried to kill Celia was gone. Yet she was here, walking through the Pavilion with them, hands covered with thin gloves so she could hug her sisters without fear. She and Jane were still debating the best way to convince their classmates that this was a new fashion trend.

"The girl underwater isn't convincing boys to buy her fondue," Jude said as they made their way down the path.

"You'd understand if you'd had that fondue. It's amazing," Jane answered wistfully.

The beach was littered with the remains of the pier. Clumps of seaweed were everywhere, though the church still stood, a temple that the ocean could never fully destroy. Underwater, things had barely changed—the storm couldn't affect something as deep as the *Glasgow*. Lo looked up at the surface, at the bits of evening sunlight filtering through the water. She turned to her sisters, the small handful who believed her, mostly young girls.

"Are you ready?" she asked, and they nodded, nervous, from the *Glasgow*'s deck. Several glanced at the cherub carvings in the railing just before they kicked off and swam to the surface, quick like dolphins, like fish, like anything born in and meant for the ocean. The ocean helped lift them up, currents pushing them toward the surface, toward the sunlight. Lo broke through first, gently. The air didn't hurt her face the way it once did, and the sunlight made her smile. She looked to the shore, to the church.

And she smiled more.

As her sisters surfaced warily around her, squinting even in the setting sun, she swam to the shore, to the people waiting there, waiting for her. She found the sand and began to walk forward. The pain in her feet was still there, growing sharper as the water grew shallower, but now she knew it was worth it.

Celia saw Lo falter, knew that the pain was growing, that her feet must be bleeding. She grabbed Jude's hand and before he could stop her, pulled him into the water. They waded to where waves splashed against their knees, Jude stiff and uncomfortable in the ocean.

Lo stood before them, listened to the whispers of her sisters, who were scared yet amazed at the same time. She craned her neck around them to see Anne and Jane, still lurking at the water's edge.

"Tell them not to worry," she said, eyes sparkling. "I promised not to drown you ages ago."

"Are you all right?" Jude asked after a few moments of the waves crashing around them.

"I am," Lo said. "I'm not afraid anymore."

"Neither am I," Celia said. She glanced back at her sisters, giggled as they loudly counted the number of ocean girls floating farther behind Lo in surprise.

"I'll be here," Lo said, and her voice dipped low, like she was worried to say this aloud. "Every other night. At seven. If you'd like. I thought you could talk with them, too," she said, looking back at her sisters. "Maybe if they know their pasts, like I did, they'll see they have a present. A future that doesn't include monsters."

"Of course," Celia said, and Lo exhaled in relief. Jude put an arm around Celia's waist, pulled her close to him and kissed the top of her head as Lo slowly backed up, still smiling, embracing the feeling of the waves around her, holding her up, loving her.

No. Not loving her. The ocean didn't love anyone. It wasn't fair, it wasn't loyal. But that didn't mean she couldn't love it anyway.

Jude and Celia retreated back to the shore, awkward and clumsy in the water, and watched as Lo and her sisters dove deep into the water. Lo swam down, down, until she was so deep that it was easy to forget there was a world above, easy to forget there were people there, wonders there, life there. Forgetting would be painless, would be simple, would be beautiful.

Yet despite it all, she chose to remember.

- Checkout Receipt -

Patron Barcode: ***********3319

Number of items: 5

Barcode: 21982027962905
Title: Fathomless /
Due: 07/11/2023

Barcode: 21982320462892
Title: Mimi and the Cutie Catastrophe /
Due: 07/11/2023

Barcode: 21982031676392
Title: Animals work /
Due: 07/11/2023

Barcode: 21982029798448
Title: The very hungry caterpillar /
Due: 07/11/2023

Barcode: 21982021895119
Title: Good enough to eat /
Due: 07/11/2023

06/20/2023 01:03:29 PM

Thurmont
301-600-7200
www.fcpl.org

- Checkout Receipt -

Barcode: 21982027962905
Title: Fathomless /
Due: 07/11/2023

Barcode: 21982320462892
Title: Mimi and the Cutie Catastrophe /
Due: 07/11/2023

Barcode: 21982031676392
Title: Animals work /
Due: 07/11/2023

Barcode: 21982029798448
Title: The very hungry caterpillar /
Due: 07/11/2023

Barcode: 21982021895119
Title: Good enough to eat /
Due: 07/11/2023

06/20/2023 01:02:53 PM

ACKNOWLEDGMENTS

Writing *Fathomless* felt a little like jumping into the ocean— you leap, and then the water is everywhere at once. One day in July, I was sitting around, and the next I was writing, plotting, revising, and obsessing—the book was everywhere at once, my entire life. I suspect it might have drowned me were it not for the help of the following people.

My agent, Jim McCarthy, and editor, Julie Scheina, for being as eager to read a new *Little Mermaid* as I was to write one.

My maternal grandparents, for taking me to Myrtle Beach as a kid, land of lemonade drinks and suntan lines, and former home of the real Pavilion.

My paternal grandparents, for taking me to Emerald Isle, a beautiful area with wild ponies, sea grass, and strong waves that remind you how small you are.

Café Jonah in Atlanta, full of incredibly nice employees

who always smiled at me, even as I took up their tables for hours on end.

Craig McClellan, for his knowledge of guitars (both pricing and sinking abilities).

Nelson Dean, for talking through the final scene even though he had no idea who Molly, Lo, or Naida were.

Maggie Stiefvater, for distracting conversations and sloth videos.

My parents and sister, for understanding when I slumped around, saying "Spoiler alert: *Everyone drowns*" for two months.